MW00941004

KILLING WITH KINGS

A GEORGIA COAST COZY MYSTERY (BOOK 4)

LOIS LAVRISA

SUNLAKE PRESS

DEDICATION

For my cousins Erik and his husband Jonathan, and Kathy and her husband Tim. I think that one of my favorite feelings is laughing with someone and realizing half way through how much you enjoy their existence.

JOIN THE NEWSLETTER

If you'd like to receive the latest news and information about my upcoming books, please sign up for my free author newsletter at:

loislavrisa.com/newsletter

CHAPTER 1

*O*fficer Nowak fumbled with her bomb squad tool kit. In the cavernous gymnasium, I stood off to the side, next to my buddy Howie, and exhaled in exasperation. Chances were good she'd fail to deactivate the explosive when the upcoming simulation exercise began. Since I was her trainer, that would be interpreted as my failure. At least this was the squad's final training day, and soon I'd be in Miami visiting my family.

Nowak wasn't my only problem. For the past week, Howie had been hinting about setting me up for a double date. So far, I'd successfully avoided the topic, but I had a feeling he was here to revisit the idea. I wanted to make sure I controlled the conversation so that I wouldn't have to answer him.

"Look who I get to train." I pointed toward Nowak.

"Rookie Nowak reminds me of Einstein's quote, 'Two things are infinite, the universe and human stupidity; and I'm not sure about the universe,'" Howie smirked. We'd met fifteen years ago in the police academy, and now Howie was a narcotics detective with the Savannah Police Department.

"Go figure. Ray makes lieutenant, and the first thing he does is dump his newbie niece on my bomb squad." I was glad Howie was allowing me to distract him.

"Nepotism sucks for you, José."

1

"She's got a fancy college degree, though, so she must be pretty smart."

"Maybe book smart. But she seems completely street stupid to me. She's as genius as Wile. E. Coyote. Might have even gotten her degree from Acme." Howie chuckled.

"Look past her overeager, reckless attitude, and I think she has the potential to be a great cop. Give her some time. I bet she'll surprise you."

"Let's hope so." Howie laughed. "By the way, for what it's worth, I think you should've gotten the promotion over Ray. You're better qualified in every way—test scores, record, and experience."

"But that doesn't seem to matter." My gut twisted anytime I heard Ray's name. He always seemed to be gunning for me. Part of me wondered if he knew I was hiding my homosexuality, and he wanted to out me in order to shame me. I wouldn't put it past him. He seemed to enjoy making himself look better at the expense of others.

"He went from sergeant to lieutenant in record time. Which leaves me to wonder who Ray's putting the screws to this time." Howie grimaced.

Years ago, Howie and I had been beat cop partners. After Howie and his wife Nicole had had their first kid, they'd begun having marital problems and decided to separate. During this time, Nicole had had an affair with Ray. The whole PD knew about it, as did half of Savannah. After counseling and mediation, Howie had reconciled with his wife, but I knew he'd never forgiven Ray. I noticed how his jaw clenched every time he spotted Ray in the same room. Sleeping with a cop's wife, either current or former, went against an unspoken hard-and-fast code.

Howie opened his arms wide. "Why can't anyone see through Ray's bullshit? Granted, he's a pretty decent cop, but c'mon, he's a horrible human being. I mean, who in the hell promotes someone like him?"

I shook my head. "Someone who has the power to slide a lame promotion by without notice."

"Maybe his dad helped him?"

"Could be. Although I don't know if he still has any influence. I guess he could. I mean, he was chief of police."

"Like, twenty years ago. But, yeah. Either it's his dad or someone on the city council. He's always kissing someone's ass." Howie mused, "Do you think it could be Patrice DeLeon who helped him?"

"I don't know for sure." I shrugged. "Nothing we can do but play the cards we're dealt." I felt torn. Yes, Ray's promotion over me had sucked, as I had been next in line for lieutenant. It would have made my dad so proud of me, his only son. The pay raise and the increased responsibilities were minor benefits compared to how happy it would have made my father. Then again, as twisted as it sounded, I was a bit relieved that I hadn't gotten the promotion. I didn't want to undergo the heightened scrutiny once I advanced. A higher rank would shine a spotlight on me and put me more in the public eye. If that ended up exposing me as a gay man, it would tear apart my safely guarded world.

Howie rubbed the top of his crew cut. "Man, if Ray were gone, I'd throw the biggest party Savannah has ever seen."

"Bigger than the Saint Patrick's Day parade?"

"That would not even come close to my celebration."

"I'd be your grand marshal." I eyed my group of trainees, all gathered and waiting for the simulated bomb exercise to begin. "You know, Ray's been a thorn in my side for years. Every chance he gets, he tries to undermine my work. He wants to make me look incompetent and ruin my career."

"Tell me something I don't know." Howie bumped my shoulder with his.

I grunted.

"Ray must really hate you," Howie added.

"Yeah, I know." I glanced over at Nowak. "Is that why you stopped by? For sheer amusement, seeing what I have to deal with?"

"Yup. I was in the area and had to get a load of this." He grinned.

"It's going to be quite a show. I have to turn her from a fumbling newbie into a freaking hero. If I can't accomplish that near-impossible feat, my flawless record of turning rookies into top-notch bomb squad officers will be in the toilet."

"Based on what I'm seeing, you've got your work cut out for you. I bet you're glad you're leaving on vacation soon. Doesn't it start in a few days?"

"Yeah. Going to Miami to see the family."

"Miami in May. It'll be pretty hot there." Howie paused, and then it came. "Hey, you're still single, right?"

I averted my eyes and nodded. "One, I have a feeling this is going to lead somewhere, and two, that's the real reason you showed up here."

"Yup. You got me on both accounts." Howie held up his hand in surrender. "So, when you get back from vacation, what do you think about going on a double date with me and my wife and her sister Janet? She's been bugging my wife about us setting you two up. Janet has the hots for you." He fanned himself as though heated. "You're both in your mid-thirties, unmarried with no kids. She's athletic, pretty, and has a great career. It's the perfect match."

I nervously laughed, shoving my sexuality deep into the pit of my stomach. It would be such a relief to be out, not to have to pretend. To be myself and therefore not get fixed up with women who thought we had a chance of being together. It was wrong. I felt like I was misleading them, playing with their hearts. I hated that feeling. I wasn't a user.

Nonetheless, I'd rather continue faking heterosexuality than face rejection and abandonment by my family and peers. I'd kept my secret at work for fear that my fellow officers might not understand and, worse, might not back me up when I needed assistance.

My phone alarm sounded, and I shut it off. Saved by the bell. Now I could avoid the Janet-date conversation. "That's my cue to start. Wish me luck."

"You don't need luck—you need a miracle," Howie called after me.

I flipped him the finger before joining my group. Four trainees had successfully completed the exercises this morning before we ran out of time and broke for lunch. Now, at the start of the afternoon session, one trainee was left. "Nowak, you're up."

"I think you gave the easier bombs to them." Nowak pointed at the four trainees behind her.

"There's no whining in the bomb squad, Nowak. And for your information"—I shook my finger side to side—"you can't *choose* which bomb you have to defuse. Get over it and focus on the task. Let me hear the bell of success and not the buzzer of failure, got it?" I hated that I'd already lost my patience with her before she'd even begun the exercise.

Nowak approached the petite, young black female actress who was sitting on a chair rigged to a bomb.

"José, you've got to be kidding me." Nowak craned her head under the chair. "Jeez, there must be fifty wires. And a pressure-sensitive bomb with a trip wire? Really?"

Her round baby face and large dark brown eyes reminded me a bit of my eldest sister, Juanita, when she was Nowak's age.

"First, what did I just say about complaining? And second, and most important, you must be under the delusion that we're equals. I'm Sergeant Rodriguez to you."

"Yes, Sergeant, sir." Nowak knelt next to the chair and opened her toolkit. "Sorry."

"*Sorry* isn't a part of our vocabulary when defusing a bomb." Maybe I'd been too hard on her.

A bead of sweat formed on Nowak's forehead. "Do I start now?"

"Unless you want your victim to get antsy and *move*." I smirked.

The actress must have taken the cue from my exchange with Nowak. She screamed, "Get me off this thing. Help me. I'm, like, ready to pass out. Oh my God, am I going to explode?"

"No. I mean, I don't *think* so," Nowak answered as she seemed to study the wires under the seat.

"You don't *think* so? Seriously? Do you even know what you're doing?" the actress asked.

"Ma'am, please *sit still* and be quiet. Any movement can set this thing off." Nowak took a deep breath as she eyed the wires.

"How in the world am I supposed to be quiet and not move? I'm freaking out, sitting on a bomb that will explode any minute. I'm going to die. We're all going to die," she cried. "Hurry up and get me off this thing before it blows!"

"I'm doing the best I can," Nowak grumbled as she pulled out a penlight from her kit. With a clatter, it fell to the floor. She retrieved it with a trembling hand.

"Then why are you dropping stuff? Holy smokes! What's taking so long?" she demanded. "I have to pee!"

"Hey, lady, knock it off," Nowak burst out. "I can't concentrate with you complaining."

The actress let out a blood-curdling, skin-prickling shriek. "There's going to be a zillion pieces of me scattered all over the room."

"Shut up," Nowak yelled.

"Oh, no, you don't." The young black woman zigzagged her finger in the air. "You're hollering at me? You're supposed to be saving me!"

"Hey, lady, I can't with you freaking out on me," Nowak returned.

"My name is Chantal, not *hey lady*. And if you haven't noticed, I'm sitting on a B-O-M-B. If there's any time to freak out, it's *now*!" she squawked.

Things were getting out of hand. I had to intervene.

"Chantal, right? That's a pretty name. Is it a family name?" I asked in my most soothing tone of voice. I made sure I made eye contact and held it. I modeled the appropriate behavior for dealing with a victim, hoping that Nowak and the other trainees took note.

"Seriously, you want to know that as I sit here one sneeze away from implosion?" Chantal, eyes red and cheeks flushed, stopped sobbing. She eyed me up and down.

My peers have told me I look like a younger version of

Dwayne Johnson. Because of this, I guess, I've had to tolerate many flirtatious women. Too bad I batted for the other team.

"I've been watching you for a while. And aren't you a gorgeous mocha-colored hot mass of muscles?" She winked at me. "Chantal is my grandmother's name."

"Well, it's a great name. Would you do me a favor, Chantal?" I asked.

"Anything for you." Chantal fluttered her eyelashes.

"Nowak is going to do her very best to get you out of this in *one piece*. Right now, the only job you have is to sit there, take deep breaths, and not move one inch off your chair. Okay, Chantal? Could you do that for me?" I placed a hand on her shoulder and felt it relax under my touch.

"As long as you don't let this klutzy cop screw it up." Chantal looked down at Nowak, whose face was inches away, next to the maze of wires connected under Chantal's chair.

"Chantal, you have my word. Sit tight a minute. Nowak, I need you for a second over here." I motioned to her.

Nowak slowly got up and stepped next to me, out of earshot of Chantal.

"You're making some big mistakes that can cost lives. First, you need to calm down your victim. If she moves a butt cheek, we'd all blow up. Got it?"

Nowak waved a hand in the direction of Chantal. "She's being such a drama queen, screaming at me and acting all crazy. I can't concentrate."

"*Poor baby.*" I narrowed my eyes at her. "Next time I'll make sure to get you a victim who's relaxed while sitting on top of a bomb. Like in *real life*."

Nowak scowled, appearing to get my sarcasm. Maybe she wasn't as dumb as Howie thought.

"But this is so much pressure, with everyone watching me and with her yelling and—" Nowak stopped midsentence, sensing that I was losing my patience.

In a calm voice, I explained, "That's why we're here. You've practiced on dozens of different IEDs in our labs and out in the field. Now you're training in a simulated real-life scenario to get you ready for the real deal out there when some jackass decides to make a bomb. That's when there will be lots of chaos, people watching, and a very terrified victim. If anything, today is a cakewalk compared to what could happen."

Nowak slumped. "Yes, Sergeant, sir."

"Concentrate. Remember what I've taught you. And if you can't handle that, just say the word, and I'll take you off the bomb squad." *Please say you want off my squad, please.*

Nowak looked down at her feet. "I want to remain on your squad, Sergeant, sir."

Damn it. "Okay, then. Get back to work."

"Yes, sir. Got it." Nowak jogged back to Chantal.

On cue, Chantal screamed at Nowak. "No more taking little chitchat breaks while my life is on the line. Get me off of here!"

Nowak took an obvious deep breath, her chest rising and falling. "I'll take care of you. I promise. What do you do, Chantal?" She knelt down again, pulling out her penlight.

I saw the light follow the wires to the detonator. Good, she appeared to have gotten rid of her nerves and was tuning in to the task at hand.

"I'm a college student," Chantal said.

"Do you have family around here?" Nowak studied the device as she spoke in a comforting voice.

"No, I don't." Chantal added, "But they'll be in town soon."

"Oh, that's good. Any special occasion?" Nowak's hand was steady as she held a wire cutter.

"Yes, for my *freaking funeral,* you moron, if you don't get me off this bomb!" Chantal screeched.

I caught myself laughing, so I turned away to avoid undermining Nowak's concentration. Glad that my pep talk had gotten her back to business, I walked over and stood next to the four rookies who were observing the simulation.

Howie sidled up to me. "Okay, this is the best one you've built yet. Before the simulation, I took a look at it. Simple but ingenious."

"Thank you." I bowed.

Howie rubbed his chin. "You have the activator, fuse, and

explosive all leading to the battery by multiple colored wires. Bet I know which one will ring the bell."

"You think so or you know so?" I asked.

"Ten bucks it's the yellow one." Howie pulled out his wallet.

I waved his outstretched hand away. "Save your money for poker."

A buzzer announced the bomb had exploded.

"Yellow was right. Too bad Nowak didn't figure that out." I punched Howie in the arm as I shouted to the trainees, "Great. We're all dead."

The other trainees snickered.

I asked, "Nowak, what went wrong?"

Nowak stood, straightening her clothes as she wiped her hands on her slacks. Her light blue T-shirt was soaked dark with sweat. "I cut the wrong wire?"

On second thought, maybe Howie was right and she was an idiot.

It took every bit of strength I had to compose myself. But I did, saying, "And let's thank our actress, Chantal."

Chantal rose and took a dramatic curtsy. "Thank you, thank you, and thank you!" She shimmied as she waved her hands over her body. "Thank goodness that was only pretend. I'd hate all of this to be scattered around."

"Let's give her a round of applause." I opened my arms wide toward Chantal.

Everyone applauded as Chantal flashed a big smile.

Howie said to the group, "And let's hear it for Sergeant Rodriguez, the finest bomb maker in Savannah—hell, the whole Southeast for that matter."

"Aren't you glad I'm on your side?" I asked. "Everyone take ten. Then we'll regroup and go over what went wrong and what Nowak should have done differently."

CHAPTER 2

A minute later I entered the men's restroom.

"But, Dad, I got the promotion." A voice rose from behind a wall divider. It sounded like Ray, only with a groveling tone rather than his typical arrogance.

"I'm still your superior. Call me sir. And it's about time, girly boy. I made chief by your age, so don't think you're anything special," came a muted voice that sounded as though it emanated from a speakerphone. "Who'd you sleep with to get it?"

"No one."

"That's hard to believe." His dad snorted.

Ray cleared his throat. "Sir, I work hard."

"Ha! That'd be a first," Ray's dad said.

"I do. Remember the guy I put away for murder for shooting a cop?"

"Yeah, I remember the cop died. That was, like, fifteen years ago. So, what about it?"

"The killer got lethal injection today. It was my case that convicted him, even though they didn't find the gun. I'm good at my job, sir. I am. I wish you'd give me credit." Ray seemed to plead his case to his father, like a child begging for a parent's approval.

"What have you done recently? You can't rest on one case."

"I don't. It's just that I thought you heard about it on the news today, and that you'd be—"

"Be what? Are you looking for an attaboy for freaking doing *your job?*"

"No, sir. It's just that I thought—"

"Are you talking back to me?"

"No, sir, I'm not. I never would." Ray's voice lowered.

"Good. Don't you ever disrespect me. Ever!"

"Sir, I gotta go." Ray sounded downtrodden.

I finished my business and then stood at the sink, washing my hands as Ray emerged from behind the divider. His eyes were red-rimmed and they widened as he spotted me. Our gazes locked.

Not knowing what to say, I nodded toward Ray, actually feeling sorry for the guy.

"What's your problem? You trying to see my junk?" Ray kicked the trash can on the way out and then slammed the door behind him.

I'd always thought that Ray could be really handsome and attractive if his personality weren't so ugly.

THE TRAINEES AND I BEGAN DEBRIEFING THE DRILL SESSION.

Ray strolled over to the group and slung an arm around his niece. "Hey, kid."

Officer Nowak beamed like a child getting attention from a parent.

Ray added, "You all keep an eye on my niece. She'll be moving up the ranks."

"More like blowing up," a trainee muttered under his breath.

The other trainees laughed.

I took a deep breath. I made a note to speak to the trainee about his inappropriate comment.

"Who said that?" Ray glared at the group.

The male trainee slowly raised his hand.

"What do you mean by that crack?" Ray demanded.

"Just that Officer Nowak failed the simulation, Lieutenant Murphy, sir. I was making light of that, sir." The trainee stood at attention, back stick straight, shoulders back, and head held high. I could almost smell the fear emanating from his pores.

Ray poked a finger toward him. With his face red, he moved within inches of the man. "You have a problem with Nowak, then you have a problem with *me*. And you never want to have a problem with me. *Ever*. Got it, *rookie?*"

"Yes, sir. I do. I'm sorry, sir." He lowered his eyes.

Looked like Ray had beaten me to the reprimand. But these were my trainees, and I was in charge of them. *Not him*.

Ray added, "I take my job seriously. I don't have time for wisecracks. I suggest you all follow suit."

The trainee mumbled something.

"Back off!" Nowak shoved the trainee. "I heard your smart-ass comment about my uncle."

The trainee pulled his hand back as though he were about to hit Nowak.

"Enough." I stepped between Nowak and the trainee. "Nowak, stand over there, and you"—I pointed toward the trainee—"keep your mouth shut. I think it's gotten you in enough trouble already."

"Obviously, you didn't listen to me when I said not to mess with my niece." Ray punched a finger at the trainee's face.

The trainee hung his head and apologized.

When he finished dressing down my trainee, I pulled Ray out of earshot of the group. "Listen, Ray, when one of my trainees steps out of line, I take care of them, not you."

"I wouldn't have to if you did your job," Ray retorted.

"You jumped in before I even had a chance to speak to him."

"Then be quicker next time." Ray turned and left.

Ray was a ticking bomb. Just as unpredictable, and just as dangerous.

CHAPTER 3

"*I* got hung up at work. Sorry I missed dinner." I plopped into one of the antique dining room chairs. It creaked with my weight. My group of friends, Bezu, Annie Mae, and Cat, sat around Bezu's dining room table. We met once a week for dinner at Bezu's house. Bezu, the gourmet cook of the group, was a genteel Southern belle. She almost always wore sundresses on her tall slender frame. Her porcelain skin was just a few shades lighter than her blond hair. Although I loved seeing my friends, it was getting more and more difficult to prevent their conversation from revolving around my secret and what I should do about it.

"What was going on at work that made you so late?" Annie Mae asked. Sixty-five and widowed, Annie Mae, a black semi-retired college professor, was by far the most outspoken of the four of us.

I took in a breath, giving me a whiff of the lingering scent of Cajun shrimp jambalaya. "I'm trying to turn a fumbling rookie into a bomb squad hero."

All that remained of the meal was dessert plates, coffee cups, and a couple of partially full wine bottles. I picked one up. "Riesling?"

"I have a merlot I could open, or I could get you a beer," Bezu offered.

"Thanks, but I don't have time."

"Where are you heading off to?" Cat asked.

"To see a buddy of mine perform at the Magnolia Club."

"Your buddy being the Sanders' Tavern bar owner, Norman?" Annie Mae asked.

I nodded. "Tonight he's Sweetie Pie, the headlining drag queen."

"What's with the frown?" Cat asked.

Not realizing that I had a tell which gave away what I was really thinking, I claimed, "Nothing." I leaned back in my chair. "Annie Mae, would you like to go with me?"

"I love live performances!" Annie Mae exclaimed, but then she raised an eyebrow. "Hey, wait. You aren't using me as a cover, are you?"

I avoided eye contact with Annie Mae. Shifting in my chair, I glanced at my phone.

"You've got to be kidding." Cat opened her arms wide. "You're still hiding? Haven't we gotten to you yet about just being you and not giving a damn what people think?"

Despite her petite, athletic build, Cat had an imposing, bigger-than-life attitude. She seemed to have unlimited energy, taking care of her two sets of twins and running a business. Besides that, she was tough.

I shrugged my shoulders.

"Good gracious, in this day and age, why don't you just come out?" Bezu folded a linen napkin.

This subject always caused my chest to tighten and gut to clench. "So, you going with me or not?" I locked eyes with Annie Mae.

"Yes. But I think you're wrong for keeping the *real you* a secret," she replied. "You gotta stop pretending to be someone you're not."

All three sets of eyes glared at me. It reminded me of when I'd get ganged up on by my three older sisters. Just like my sisters, these women weren't going to back off.

I put a hand up. "The police department is different. It's a brotherhood."

"So?" Annie Mae raised an eyebrow.

"Trust me. They wouldn't get it." I looked down at the floor.

"What I don't get is why you're being such a weirdo about this. In today's world, I think people are way more open-minded, with all the media coverage on LGBTQ acceptance and all. Mind you, a decade ago, that wasn't the case," Annie Mae said. "But you should have no problem coming out now."

"Not to my peers. If I tell them I'm gay, I bet I'll have people ignoring my calls for backup." I stood, hoping that would end the conversation. "It's complicated."

"I've been telling you this for years, I think your excuse is catawampus." Bezu tucked a strand of blond hair behind her ear. "I think we are right, but I will respect your decision, *for now.*"

The others nodded in agreement.

"Time to go." I held my hand out to help Annie Mae stand from her chair.

"Such a gentleman." Annie Mae accepted my hand. "I'm looking forward to some entertainment. I'm going to party until I drop."

"Something tells me I'm going to regret taking you." I grinned as I pushed in the empty chair.

"I don't know what you're talking about." Annie Mae patted her short black hair. "I'm an angel."

"An angel with horns who sticks her nose where it doesn't belong." I shook my head, still smiling.

"I have no idea what you are referring to." She smoothed her blue silk shirt over her black dress slacks. "I don't stick *anything* where it doesn't belong."

"Oh, you don't? I remember what happened at your last summer theater camp."

"Who could forget that? She solved *two* murders," Bezu said.

"Yes, I did. And before that, you solved one, Bezu," Annie Mae replied. "I'd say we are quite the amateur sleuths."

I let out a long, deep breath. They thought just because they happened to have been successful, it meant they were skilled at what they did. Sure, they were all intelligent, very competent ladies, and I loved them like my own sisters. But they were not trained police. What they didn't realize was that their so-called crime solving had amounted to a lot of luck. Had one thing gone the wrong way, they could've died.

"And one for me, too." Cat held up her hand with her thumb tucked in. "That's four altogether. You got to admit, that's pretty good."

I pointed at all of them. "I *prevent* murders by defusing bombs. So *I win*."

"But we are good, you have to admit that. I think us gals should form our own detective agency," Annie Mae declared, high-fiving Bezu and Cat.

"*No* way, *no how* is that a good idea. Wipe that from your minds." I felt my neck stiffen and my veins stick out. They thought it was a joke, but each one of them had nearly died. I would never forgive myself if anything ever happened to any of them.

I lowered my voice's volume. "I'm going to say this one last time. Stay out of police business. Got it? End of subject." I put my left elbow akimbo. "Let's go, Annie Mae."

She threaded her arm through mine. "Okay, grumpy pants. But you better change your attitude. 'Cause I'm gonna have a hoot tonight. Just watch me." Annie Mae wiggled her full figure. "All this is going to have a great time."

CHAPTER 4

*A*nnie Mae and I entered the Magnolia Club just as speakers blasted the last chorus of "I Will Survive." The wall-to-wall tables were packed, and those who couldn't find seats lined up at the back bar. Strobe lights punctuated the darkened room. The air was thick with the smell of stale beer and bargain perfume.

Applause saluted the Diana Ross drag queen, who exited behind the red velvet curtain.

The announcer on stage said, "Thank you, Delightful D. Ross, for that incredible performance. Now, for the debut of her new act, let's all give it up for Savannah's Southern-fried and sassy, always entertaining, the one and only Sweetie Pie."

"Looks like we got here just in time," I told Annie Mae. We threaded our way through the crowd to a small table near the stage with a reserved sign.

The pounding rhythms of "It's Raining Men" filled the room as Sweetie Pie, looking fit, lip-synced and danced around the stage.

At one point, Sweetie Pie came out into the audience to mingle with the crowd, who hooted and shouted their approval. Upon arriving at my table, she wrapped a fuchsia feather boa around my neck. My chest squeezed. I felt the urge to duck out before anyone could see me getting singled out.

At that very moment, I saw Ray standing off to the side. We made eye contact.

I turned my back to him. When Sweetie Pie finally exited the stage, I touched Annie Mae's arm. "I'm going to the bar. Can I get you anything?"

"Something sweet and salty like me," she answered.

"Margarita it is."

"I'll meet you there, but I have to go to the ladies' room first." Annie Mae stood.

I made my way to the bar and placed my order.

A minute later, Ray was next to me. "I know why *I'm* here."

"And why are you here?"

"Not that I have to tell you, but I'm checking IDs, making sure the place isn't serving minors. So why are you here?"

I felt my stomach clench. "I'm watching a friend perform."

"I don't see any *performers* here." Ray snickered.

I held back the urge to haul off and hit him.

The bartender put the drinks in front of me. I noticed he was tall and thin, clean-shaven but with long hair. He next placed a bowl of nuts beside the drinks.

"Jeez! Get these away from me," Ray screamed.

The bartender grabbed the bowl just as another patron reached an arm in front of him, causing the nuts to flip over onto Ray.

"Idiot!" Ray grabbed his throat as he jammed a hand into the pocket of his battered leather jacket. He yanked out an EpiPen. Sweat beaded on Ray's forehead as he clutched onto the bar, his chest visibly rising and falling. A few moments later, he put the unused device back in his pocket.

"Are you all right?" I asked. Even though I didn't like him, he was obviously in distress.

"I'll shut this place down! And fire you!" Ray shouted at the bartender, ignoring my question.

The bartender's eyes were wide.

Looking at the bartender, I said, "Ignore him." Then I turned to Ray. "What's your problem? It's not like you're wearing a sign around your neck that says you're allergic to peanuts. How in the hell is he supposed to know?"

Ray glared at the bartender. "He's lucky I didn't go into anaphylactic shock."

The bartender shook his head as he wiped the countertop.

Barking at him, Ray ordered, "Get me a glass of water."

"Doesn't it get exhausting?" I asked Ray.

"What?" He raised an eyebrow.

"Being *you*," I replied.

"I don't know what you're referring to. I'm just doing my job. More than I can say for you." Ray huffed as he grabbed the glass of water from the bartender. He took a chug.

A man with a thick build and auburn hair came over to us, apparently the bouncer. "Legally, you can come in and check IDs," the man told Ray. "But you're not allowed to berate anyone. I think you need to head on out the door."

"Did you just give me an order? I'm here on official business, and you have no right to tell me when I have to go." Ray puffed out his chest and set down his glass.

"For months now you've been trying to find us in violation of *whatever*, and you haven't. So why don't you just leave us alone?" The bouncer stood chest to barrel chest with Ray.

The veins on Ray's neck stood out as he shoved a barstool away. It looked like he wanted to punch the bouncer. "I can get you fired! I've done it before, and I can do it again."

The bouncer squared his shoulders as though he were preparing for battle.

Needing to defuse the tense situation and avoid a brawl, I slid between Ray and the bouncer. "Hey, Ray, let's take a step back. Enjoy the show."

"I'm not done with you," Ray snarled at the bouncer.

"I've got this," I told the bouncer.

The man nodded.

Ray changed his stance as he glared at the bouncer.

"Leave it alone, Ray. Relax." I held my hands up.

"You got my drink?" Annie Mae had joined us. She took a

quick glance at Ray, looked toward the bouncer, and then back at me. "What's going on here? Looks like a rumble is about to break out."

"Nothing," I claimed.

The bouncer nodded toward me and then walked back to his post at the nearby door.

Ray grabbed his glass of water and emptied it.

I handed Annie Mae her drink.

Sweetie Pie walked over to us. "I heard someone's messing with my bartender friend, Elias."

Elias smiled at Sweetie Pie as he filled a mug from the beer tap. He shot a glance toward Ray.

"It's under control," I claimed.

Sweetie Pie wrapped her pink feather boa around Ray's neck. "It looks like I'm not the only drama queen here."

Overhearing Sweetie Pie's comment, several bystanders clapped.

"Get this crap off me." Ray untangled himself from the feathers. "You need to back off me, *whatever* you are."

"Oh, I could say so much back to you." Sweetie Pie winked at Ray. "But in a battle of wits, it would be wrong to attack someone who's totally unarmed."

"Trust me, I'm armed, and don't you forget it." Ray stomped away.

Sweetie Pie called after Ray, "I love the sound you make when you shut up."

CHAPTER 5

"Thanks for being here with me," Bezu said as we stood outside City Hall. We'd just finished filling out the application for her building permit. "Aren't you supposed to be on vacation soon? I know you didn't need to be here, but I'm glad for the moral support wrangling all this paperwork."

"Glad to help. And, yes, I started vacation today. I've got a few days in town before I leave to visit my folks and sisters in Miami. So, when does construction start on your kitchen?"

"I've been busier than a moth in a mitten getting that all together." Bezu pulled her long blond hair back into a ponytail. "Trying to install modern kitchen equipment in an 1893 house is proving to be very challenging."

"I bet. But knowing you, it'll be great when it's done." I paused and asked, "What does your fiancé think about the renovation?"

"Luiz is concerned that I'm spending so much time on it." Bezu ran a finger along her pearl necklace. "He said I should just open my own restaurant instead of doing all the work on the house in order to run my catering business there."

"Why don't you open a place?"

Bezu took in a long breath. "Cooking in my own home makes me feel like my family is with me, even if just in spirit.

Also, I have no desire to run a restaurant. I'd lose the personal, homemade touch that clients have told me makes my food stand out from the rest."

"You gotta do what's best for you. Sounds like you know that."

People were filing out of the building onto the street. Out of the corner of my eye, I saw Earl Chu. He had distinctive high cheekbones, a square jaw, and pitch-black hair. I'd seen him around the courthouse. He was a well-respected public defense attorney. We'd exchanged greetings but nothing beyond that.

"He's cute, huh?" Bezu remarked.

I hadn't realized I was staring. "Don't know who you're talking about." When I heard my name being called, I turned and saw Patrice DeLeon, a city councilwoman. She was waving at me. "Will you excuse me?" I asked Bezu.

"You go on ahead. I have to meet with my architect. I'll see you tonight at the poker tournament?"

She had been hired to cater dinner for the group. "What are you making?"

"Easy finger food. Sandwiches, homemade chips, my special secret recipe pickles, and for dessert, muffins." Bezu hugged me. Before she turned and walked away, she said, "I hope you win big."

"That's my plan."

Patrice DeLeon greeted me. "She's very pretty. Is she your girlfriend?"

Shaking my head no, I avoided belaboring the topic by asking my own question. "How are you? I haven't seen you in a while."

"I'm great." She undid the top button of her blazer. Her neck looked flushed. "I wanted to congratulate you for making it to the final table."

"Thank you. And back at you."

She smiled. "I look forward to playing."

"So do I. More importantly, I look forward to winning."

"Me, too. But there can only be one champion."

"You're looking at him."

She shook her head and grinned. "No, I think you're looking at the winner right now."

I pulled out my phone so that I could see my reflection. "Yes, I am."

We both laughed.

I always had liked her. She seemed like a decent, hardworking politician, and I had always considered her a friend. However, after overhearing the conversation between Ray and his dad, I could almost guarantee it wasn't his father who'd arranged Ray's promotion.

On occasion, I had seen Patrice and Ray together. I'd always assumed their meetings were professional, since all she seemed to boast about in the media was her happy marriage any chance the press was around. Still, their relationship, whatever it was, made me think that Patrice might have been the one who had something to do with Ray's promotion. The idea irked me to no end. But I knew she had clout, and it was best to remain friendly and professional and not let my personal feelings get in the way.

"Don't you think that you and I are evenly matched?" She slid her large black-rimmed sunglasses down, exposing her hazel eyes. Her large multi-diamond wedding ring glistened in the sun. "Judging by the rest of the table, we're the ones to beat. Except Ray has been a really strong player in the games leading up to the tournament. He might surprise us."

"We'll find out tonight," I replied. "Meanwhile, how's your reelection campaign coming along?"

She was currently running for a second term as city councilwoman. Everyone knew, however, that she had her political ambitions set on the state legislature. Her campaign focused on her strong morals. Her slogan was "Always doing what's right." If she had gotten Ray the promotion, I found this ironically amusing.

"Good. But until my constituents vote, no one knows for sure."

"I think you'll win by a landslide, *again*," I claimed.

"So, what were you doing here today?" Patrice asked me.

"Giving moral support to my friend. She's applying for a building permit."

"If she needs help, please let me know. I have some favors I can call in."

"Thanks. I appreciate it."

"Hey." She reached out to grab my shoulder. "I'm really sorry you didn't get the promotion. You deserved it."

I wanted to scream at her. My suspicion was strong that she'd called in favors in order to get Ray promoted over me. *Yes, I did deserve it, and I should have gotten it instead of Ray. What were you thinking? How could you do that? I thought we were friends!* My gut tightened. My jaw clenched as I took in a deep breath. "I'll see you tonight, then?"

"Yes, as the new champion." She laughed as she waved a hand in the air and strolled away.

CHAPTER 6

*S*anders' Tavern's owner, Norman, aka Sweetie Pie, greeted me as I entered the bar. He wore a plaid button-down shirt and jeans.

We were the only two people at the entrance. Everyone else was gathered near the back of the long, rectangular room. I poked his Oxford-shirted chest. "I kind of miss your pink boa and beehive wig."

Norman laughed. "Here, I'm just a dive bar owner. I like to keep my professional life and personal life separate."

"By the way, you've trimmed down a lot, haven't you? I noticed it the other night at the club."

"Yup. Twenty pounds lighter. Heart doctor said if I didn't lose the weight, my ticker would kill me." He tapped his chest. "Although I hate exercise, I've been running three miles a day for the past few months."

"Good for you." I smiled.

"So, do you feel lucky tonight?" Norman locked the door behind me. The tavern was closed to the public tonight in order to host the poker tournament.

"Absolutely." I carried a jacket and wore my lucky blue T-shirt with faded white lettering that said, "I see guilty people," both an ode to my favorite movie, *The Sixth Sense*, and a nod to my career.

"Weird weather huh? One day it's hot and humid, and then today we get a cold snap."

"To paraphrase Mark Twain, if you don't like the weather now, just wait a few minutes."

"Isn't that the truth." Norman motioned toward the back wall, near the exit door and restrooms, where a few other coats already hung. "You're welcome to hang your jacket back there."

"Will do."

"You're the last of the players to arrive." He paused for a moment and locked eyes with me. "Lieutenant Ray Murphy seems to be on his best behavior tonight."

"Oh?"

"You should have seen the way he greeted me, like we were long-lost buddies. You'd never guess he's been such a pain in my backside for so long. Everyone knows we can barely tolerate each other." Norman sneered. "He was so nice it took me aback."

"He has his moments." I smiled.

"On the other hand, he could be playing head games as a competitive move."

I waved a hand. "I think we'll all do whatever it takes to win the pot tonight."

"I heard tonight's kitty is at five thousand?"

I nodded.

Norman leaned in, "Between you and me, I hope you get it all."

I grinned. "I bet you said that to every player tonight."

"What can I say?" Norman shrugged his shoulders smiled. "Oh, and we lucked out. Your dealer tonight used to work in Vegas. The big league."

"How did you find her?"

"She's the sister of a friend of mine at the Magnolia Club."

"As long as she gives me all the winning cards." I winked.

A knock at the door made both Norman and me turn.

Norman looked through the peephole and unlocked the door. After he opened it, we greeted Bezu.

"Good evening, gentlemen." Bezu held a large wicker basket in one hand and had a bag slung over her shoulder. "I hope you like what I made for you."

I took the basket from her. "I know I will."

"Thanks, I really appreciate it." Norman kissed her cheek. "One day you'll be so popular you won't have time to cater small jobs like this."

"My britches will never get too big to help out friends," Bezu disagreed. "Where would you like me to set up?"

Norman pointed toward the bar.

"Please don't mind me. I'll get this taken care of. Y'all go and play." Bezu began to unload items from her bag.

AT THE BACK OF THE LONG ROOM, IN PLACE OF THE USUAL SMALL round tables, stood one large oval table topped with green felt. The five other players in the tournament socialized in their seats.

As I approached the group, I greeted Patrice, Ray, and Howie. Then I shook hands with the other players, people I'd met at one time or another during previous rounds in the tournament: twenty-something-year-old firefighter JJ and the eldest of the group, prominent personal injury attorney Dickey.

Norman announced, "This here's our professional dealer, Maggie. She used to work in Vegas, but she's moved to Savannah and is now working on gambling boats around this area."

"Nice to meet you." I shook the dealer's perfectly manicured hand.

"And over there, serving as my helper, is Big Mike." Norman pointed toward the guy at the bar, whom I recognized from the other night as the bouncer at the Magnolia Club.

Big Mike walked over to the table. "Can I take your drink orders?"

"Oh? So you're working here now?" Ray addressed Big Mike. "Must be because you lost your other job as a bouncer."

Big Mike folded his arms on his chest.

Ray's eyes narrowed into a squint. "That'll teach you to mess with me."

"No. It teaches me that you're abusing your power, that's what." Big Mike's posture stiffened.

Ray shoved his chair out, making a loud scraping noise on the floor. He stood and moved nose to nose with Big Mike. "You still have a job here, so be grateful."

"Okay. Enough, guys. Cool it," JJ interjected. "How 'bout we get the game going soon?"

"Yeah, cut out whatever BS you have going on," Dickey said to them.

Big Mike shook his head, as if in resignation.

Ray huffed and sat down.

"Oh, and you"—Dickey pointed to Big Mike—"tell Norman I'd like a scotch with a splash of Coke, on the rocks. Make that *two*."

As Big Mike took our drink orders, the air remained tense from the verbal tussle. I shook it off, refusing to get caught up in any drama.

For several minutes, we chatted amongst ourselves. During this time, Norman made the drinks, and then Big Mike delivered them.

Looking at the beer-themed neon wall clock, I saw it was still a few minutes before our start time. I wiped the palms of my hands on the top of my jeans.

"Can you turn on the air, please?" Patrice called out to Norman.

"Will do." Norman nodded and walked away.

The temperature outside had a slight chill, in the midsixties, but the tavern felt warm and stuffy.

Patrice fanned herself with her hand.

"It sounds like hot flashes or something?" Howie asked Patrice.

"You're always such a gentleman, Howie." Patrice grinned.

"Sorry, that was out of line. It just slipped out. My sister-in-law is going through early menopause, and all I hear about is her body temperature, too hot or too cold. It's never just right," Howie explained.

"No harm done at all," Patrice assured him.

"So, how long have you been a dealer?" Ray looked at Maggie.

She glanced toward him. "Quite a while." Then she winced and rubbed her fingertips on her temples.

My mom wore a similar expression when she had the start of a headache.

"Don't you trust that Norman found us a reputable one?" Patrice asked.

"I was just trying to make conversation with her," Ray offered.

"How hospitable of you, Ray." Patrice then addressed Maggie. "I, for one, just want to know who does your nails. They are simply flawless. Much prettier than mine. Look what my nail tech talked me into." She held up her red-white-and-blue-painted nails.

"Ladies, I think you both are lovely, but this is not a beauty salon. Can we get this game going?" Dickey took a swig of his drink.

"What are you in a hurry for? Is there another accident you need to get to?" Howie chuckled.

"Hey. I don't only do PI cases." Dickey lifted his chin. "Do you need a will?"

"Nope. But I do need my tree cut down. Can you bring your axe?" Howie snickered.

"So you like the new commercial?" Dickey asked.

"It's a bit over the top," JJ put in.

"But it got me noticed. I've got a director calling about a reality show. If you're nice, I might let you all be in it." Dickey swished the ice in his raised glass.

"No, thanks. Not for me," Patrice said.

"I'll pass on that, too. Not sure that's the type of exposure I want," JJ agreed.

"Really? *Mr. February?* I thought you'd jump all over that," Howie said.

"You're jealous we have the most popular calendar in Savannah." JJ smirked. "Cops don't have a calendar."

"'Cause we're too busy *working* instead of posing." Howie chortled.

I had to laugh, too.

"Thanks, but no thanks," Ray added. "No offense, but the last thing I want is to be associated with a two-bit reality TV show about a gimmicky attorney."

"No harm, no foul, Ray." Dickey sat back in his chair. "Just remember when the show makes it big that I gave you all an opportunity to get in on it."

"Duly noted." I grinned.

Ray sat to the left of the dealer. On the other side of Maggie was JJ. I had taken the only empty chair, which put me right between Howie and Patrice.

Maggie took a new deck of cards from Norman and held them up for all of us to see that they were sealed. She cut them open. After she dispersed the chips, she fanned out the cards on the table, then flipped, shuffled, and cut them.

"Let's roll," Ray said.

"Get ready to lose," JJ responded.

"You're kidding me, right?" Ray smirked. "That coming from someone whose entire job can be replaced by *water*."

JJ rolled his eyes. "Pizza delivery arrives quicker than the police."

"Watch it, JJ, you're outnumbered here." I admired JJ's spunk, and it didn't hurt that he was a really nice guy. But there were three cops in the room.

"God made police so firemen would have heroes," Howie quipped.

"JJ, I warned you. Do you want to keep going?" I grinned.

JJ held up his hand in defeat as he chuckled. "I'm done, *for now*."

"Boys, boys. What am I going to do with you all?" Patrice dabbed her forehead with a napkin. "There is way too much testosterone in this room. Can you all rein it in and channel it to poker?" She smiled, adding, "And watch me win."

"I hate to disappoint you, but I'll be taking home all the cash." Ray folded his arms over his chest.

"No, Ray, that would be me. I feel luckier than I ever have." Dickey waved his drink. "You all can just hand over your chips to me now and go home."

"Ha! Over my dead body," Ray snorted.

CHAPTER 7

"*O*kay, then, ten bucks." Ray called the small blind bet and pushed his chips toward the middle, nearly knocking over Dickey's drink.

"Twenty bucks." Dickey slid his corresponding chips in for the big blind. "By the way, any of you need a power of attorney? I've got some time on my hands and could cut you a great deal."

Dickey never gave up. I had to admire his tenacity. I also couldn't help but wonder if his fourth divorce had strained his finances.

"I could cut my hourly rate in half. But the offer only stands this week," Dickey continued.

"Thanks for the generous offer, but I'm good," Patrice said. "Okay, the blinds are out. Let's move on."

Maggie dealt clockwise, giving each player one card at a time until each of us had two.

"Call." Patrice put in the requisite number of chips.

Looking at my hole cards, I saw a seven-two off suit. It was a miserable starting hand. "Fold," I announced and hoped my cards the rest of the night would be better than my first hand. If not, I could kiss the five-thousand-dollar kitty goodbye.

"Raise." Howie's eyes didn't blink while he slid in chips.

JJ's forehead glistened with a slight sheen of sweat. He

twisted his mouth, as though trying to decide what to do next. He paused before admitting, "I'm out."

Ray placed his cards facedown in front of him and folded his hands over them.

I guessed that Ray had a good hand by the way he protected his cards with his hands held over them. His lips tightened in a thin line. His eyes averted toward the dealer.

"Call." Ray leaned forward slightly as he moved one hand to place his bet.

Dickey's hand shook ever so faintly as he drank his scotch and soda on the rocks. Although his outward signs of age, including his sun-spotted and wrinkled skin, might cause some players to discount him as a threat, I knew better. "Fold." Dickey set down his drink and then threaded a hand through his thick white hair.

Patrice pushed more chips in. "Call."

After the preflop betting ended, Maggie dealt the flop, placing the top card in the deck facedown on the table, followed by three cards face up. Another round of betting started for the three remaining players.

Patrice tapped her long fingers on the table as she looked around the room through her thick black-rimmed glasses. "Check."

The last time I'd lost to her, she'd beaten me on the river, pure luck on her part.

"Check." Howie kept his expression neutral. Having been his beat partner, I knew him through and through. This was good inside knowledge to have as a player against him in the game. Then again, he could read me just as well.

"Bet." Ray smiled ear to ear. "I'm just getting warmed up. Why don't we end this now, and you all just hand over all your chips?"

"Good idea. Push them my way, Ray. Call." Howie glanced at the other cop's stack. "I'll be taking them all from you before long."

"You both think you have good hands?" Patrice slowly slid

more chips into the pot. "Don't get too cocky. Those might be the only good cards you have all night. Call."

"Or they could be the first of many." Ray stole a glance at Maggie. She caught his eye, and he grinned.

Maggie dealt two more cards.

Was he flirting with her?

Patrice won that hand. For the next hour, we played several more hands. Dickey, JJ, and Howie had multiple losses, which were reflected in their dwindling stacks. Patrice won the most pots, followed by me and then Ray.

We had just finished a hand when Norman came over to the table. "Is now a good time for you all to take a break? The food is ready."

"It's a perfect time." Patrice slung her purse over her shoulder.

"I'm ready for a break," I agreed.

"Might as well." Dickey stood. "I need to stretch my legs and rub a lucky rabbit foot. Heck, the whole damn rabbit, for that matter, as cruddy as my cards have been."

I didn't want to say that maybe his fortune might change if he took it easy on the scotch and sodas.

"I have to use the restroom." JJ stretched his arms over his head. "And I might actually consider leaving out the back door and running away before I lose my shirt."

I laughed. "You're not doing so bad."

"But not so good, either," JJ replied.

Maggie fanned the cards on the table and then gathered her purse and sweater. She made her way to the back by the restrooms.

Howie and Dickey chatted near the table while Ray and I headed to the bar area. Bezu had set out plates and silverware, napkins, sandwiches, chips, potato salad, pickles, and a tray of muffins.

Ray moved next to Bezu, who was putting containers away in her basket. "Hello, there," he told her. "Thanks for making us dinner tonight. I really appreciate it."

"You are more than welcome," Bezu replied. "I'm honored to do it."

"I read the article in *Savannah* magazine about you. By the way, they took great pictures of you. You looked like a super-model. And you do in person, too."

Bezu blushed and stepped back. With an ear-to-ear grin, she looked at him and said, "Why, thank you. I will let my fiancé know that he's not alone in his favorable estimation of me."

"He's a lucky guy," Ray told her.

"I hope you enjoy the meal, Ray." Bezu smiled.

"Thank you. I'm sure I will."

Dickey sauntered over to Bezu and leaned on the counter next to her, clearly violating her personal space. "You know, it's hard to find a woman who's good in the kitchen and looks good, too."

Bezu laughed. "Then you must not be looking in the right places."

For once, Dickey seemed at a loss for words. He retreated to the spot where the others were plating their food.

I gave Bezu a thumbs-up. Her cordial comebacks were one of the many qualities I loved about her.

Bezu pulled her shoulders back, tucked a strand of her long blond hair behind her ear, and curtsied.

I laughed out loud.

CHAPTER 8

A while later, we were back at the table.

Big Mike collected empty glasses and delivered fresh drinks to each of us. I thanked him as he set down my beer.

Maggie dealt the cards.

Howie looked at his hand and then nodded slightly.

Ray looked at his cards, placed them facedown, and rubbed his mouth. "The poker gods are looking down on me. Patrice, I'm knocking you out of the lead."

Dickey peeled up a corner of his cards, cocked his head, and looked at them. "Hold off there, big-shot Ray. I think my luck has changed." His words sounded marginally slurred. He finished off his drink and waved to Big Mike to bring another.

"And mine, too," Howie said.

"Fortune is with me, as well." Patrice placed her elbows on the table.

"I've got the best hand of the night," I claimed.

"*You wish.*" Ray scratched his arm.

"Yeah, I'm not falling for that." JJ smirked. "You're all bluffing."

"Am I?" Dickey raised an eyebrow.

"Yeah, hose jockey, why don't you try me?" Ray coughed and then took a sip of his beer.

"You want to mess with my head, and it won't work." JJ tapped his facedown cards.

"Won't it?" Ray's voice sounded hoarse. Sweat formed on his upper lip.

Howie interjected, "You know what they say, JJ. If you want your cat saved, call a fireman; if you want your life saved, call a cop."

"Really, Howie, you want in on this?" JJ smirked. "I guess you have no choice. It takes two cops to equal one fireman."

Howie held up his glass as if in surrender. "Touché, smoke eater. Touché."

I always enjoyed hearing the ribbing between cops and firemen. "Not your best there, Ray. I think you could do better."

Ray rubbed his throat. "JJ, maybe you should quit poker and go back to doing your difficult job: *climbing ladders*."

"Really, Ray, you want to talk about jobs?" JJ shot back. "I heard you arrested the Energizer bunny and charged him with battery."

We all laughed.

"Okay, boys, are you going to play or what?" Patrice asked. "'Cause I feel like I'm sitting in the schoolyard with a bunch of children trying to out-smack-talk each other."

"I'm ready." I had pocket aces. A great hand. This night had taken a turn for the better. I could almost feel my victory.

"Then let's play." Howie straightened his back.

Coughing and wheezing, Ray let his cards fall from his hand. He jumped up, bumping the table as his chair toppled with a bang. His cell phone clattered to the floor. He was shaking as he held his stomach.

Dickey looked at the cards Ray had dropped. "Damn, Ray. *Two kings*."

Ray stumbled to the back wall. He reached in a pocket of his hanging coat and pulled out an EpiPen. He popped it open and then jammed it into his left thigh.

"What's going on?" Dickey asked.

I stood. "He's having an allergic reaction!"

Everyone looked at Ray.

Ray had one hand on the wall as he doubled over coughing.

"Sounds like he's gasping for air," Dickey pointed out. "How long does the shot take to work?"

"Right away," I said. Every cell in my body stood at alert, ready to pounce into action if needed.

Ray slumped to the ground.

I rushed over to Ray's supine body and checked his pulse, which was faint. His breathing was labored. I immediately began CPR with chest compressions. His chest was sweaty, his breathing shallow, and his skin pale. As I tipped his head back to open his airway, his skin felt clammy.

JJ made it to my side. "Let me give it a try."

I stood and quickly called 911, giving them my badge number, location, and details of what had happened.

"Why is the medicine taking so long to work?" Dickey set his drink on the table.

I began to panic inside. I had the very same question.

By this time, everyone had left the table.

Bezu was at my side, her hand on my arm. "Ray ate *my food.*"

"We all did."

"But none of you are having issues except Ray." Bezu's voice shook. "José, maybe it's my fault."

I put a hand on her shoulder. "No, it's not. If it had anything to do with your food, which it did not, he would have reacted immediately."

"But what if he had some type of delayed reaction?" Bezu bit her bottom lip. "I was careful when I made the food. Really, I was. I followed everyone's dietary needs and took note of any allergies. Dickey no dairy, Ray no peanuts, Patrice gluten-free bread." Bezu breathed deeply and hung her head. "José, I wiped the kitchen counters down. I wore gloves, I—I—"

"It's okay." I locked eyes with her.

"You think so?" Bezu asked.

"Yes, trust me."

Patrice stood near Maggie.

JJ called out, "His mouth and throat are swollen, and he's not getting any air. He's unresponsive."

Ray's eyes stared unmoving at the ceiling. Why wasn't the epinephrine shot working?

JJ continued chest compressions.

The siren of an ambulance neared. Norman opened the front door and let the paramedic and EMT in. As they worked on Ray, everyone gathered off to the side.

We all seemed to hold our collective breath as we watched.

A few minutes later, JJ walked over to me. "They can't do an endotracheal intubation because his throat is closed. They're going to have to do a tracheostomy."

"That bad?" Howie said.

"Yes. But the good news for Ray is that this team has experience doing the procedure," JJ added.

"Good," I said. How had this gone from bad to worse so quickly?

The room felt colder and seemed darker than it had a few minutes before. We all stood and continued to watch. The air felt charged.

As I observed the paramedics working on Ray, something gnawed at me. I couldn't wrap my mind around Ray's lack of response to the epinephrine. It usually took effect in seconds. It had been a few minutes now.

Howie sidled next to me. "I called his niece and let her know what's going on. She's on her way here."

I didn't like Ray, and that was a known fact. But he was in serious trouble, and I hated that the CPR I'd performed hadn't worked, and now I couldn't do anything but stand by and wait.

Howie added, "I'm sure he'll be fine any minute. Back to his annoying self in no time."

I grinned. "You got that right." My body tensed as my pulse quickened. I hated not doing anything. Not being able to help when someone was in trouble made me anxious. Surely the epinephrine will do its job and Ray will be fine.

A few moments later, the paramedics stopped working on Ray. One stood followed shortly by the other. Their equipment lay strewn on the floor near Ray.

"We did all we could." One of the paramedics looked at me and then at Howie. "He's dead."

Dead? I felt completely unmoved. I wasn't proud of that. What I felt instead of sadness was irritation, as if I had a stone in my shoe. Only this stone was in my thoughts. Why hadn't the EpiPen worked? How had Ray gotten exposed to the allergen? And what triggered Ray's allergy so quickly?

Maggie held a hand to her head as if she were ready to faint. Bezu went to her and put her arm around her. Patrice looked shocked; her mouth hung open, and she hugged herself.

Norman paced in front of the bar. "Oh, shit."

Mike shook his head as he put a hand on the counter as if to support himself.

"Why didn't he respond to the shot?" Dickey called out.

"I don't know." I felt like a weight sat on my shoulders. I needed to take charge of the situation, secure the area. "No one touch anything until the police get here. They'll definitely want to bag the EpiPen and then probably search the entire place."

"José, I was just going to ask someone to do that," Dickey agreed. "If that shot didn't work like it was supposed to, then it could be a faulty product."

I took a long breath, irritated with Dickey. "I know how to do my job."

"This could be a huge lawsuit," Dickey added.

"C'mon. Back off, a guy just died," I told him. Even though Ray was a jerk, he still deserved a little respect.

"Now, hold on there. I have sympathy. Really, I do. But I also want to preserve his legal rights." Dickey raised an eyebrow. "I need to get a hold of Ray's family. Do you know any of them?"

I didn't know Ray's father but could guess what he was like after overhearing their conversation the other day. Meanwhile, two policemen walked in. I told Dickey, "There's Officer Nowak, Ray's niece."

Officer Nowak and Homicide Detective McFalls made their way to us.

I leaned in toward Dickey. "I would tread lightly here. I wouldn't be jumping to conclusions."

Dickey tilted his head and held up a hand. "I'm a professional."

I continued, "None of us knows what really happened. Neither of us have all the facts."

Dickey glanced at me. "I'm just saying, if it turns out to be wrongful death, I need to be there to help his family."

Dickey was acting like an ambulance-chasing lawyer, which annoyed me to no end. I put my hands in the air. "Dickey, do what you gotta do. I'm gonna do my job."

Dickey greeted Nowak with an outstretched hand. "I'm sorry for your loss. I want you to know I will do everything in my power to help you."

CHAPTER 9

*W*hile Dickey talked nearby with Nowak and McFalls, Howie and I waited by the bar.

Howie leaned against the counter. "Do you believe this? Ray is *gone*."

"No. It still hasn't sunk in yet that he's gone."

"I know. I think we're all shock," Howie glanced around the room. "I can't believe he died."

I lowered my voice. "Between you and me, I think there's more to this than an accident."

"Really? 'Cause I think there's *nothing* more to this. It was a tragedy, pure and simple." Howie ran a hand through his hair. "A *freak* one at that."

"I don't think so."

"Oh?"

"Yeah, there's something *off* about it."

"Like what?" Howie asked.

I answered even as Nowak and Dickey came up next to us. "How did Ray get exposed to peanuts in the first place? And why didn't the EpiPen work? He got worse instead of better."

Dickey joined our conversation. "Sorry about eavesdropping, but I gotta jump in here. I can understand why Ray didn't get better. There's a recall on EpiPens. Faulty auto injectors."

Howie rolled his eyes. "Why am I not surprised you know that?"

"It's my public service responsibility to stay up-to-date on product recalls." Dickey glanced at Nowak. "Plus, I just Googled it."

Nowak started to weep. "So if my uncle had one of those bad ones, instead of working and saving him, it might have killed him?"

Dickey handed her a business card. "It could be a case of product liability. Put me to work, and I'll help you *chop through legal issues.*"

Nowak sobbed as her body shuddered. "I heard my uncle was having an allergic reaction, so I wanted to be here with him. I had no idea that I'd come here and he'd be *dead.*" She let out a loud wail.

Bezu rushed to Nowak's side, putting an arm around her and guiding her to a chair.

"Poor kid. It's a tough situation she's in. I gotta make some calls." Dickey waved as he turned and walked off.

Once Dickey and Nowak were out of earshot, I told Howie, "I'm not sure anyone should leave."

"Hold on there, José," McFalls said, apparently overhearing. "This is my call. I'm in charge here. And this is *not* a crime scene. *Everyone is free to go.* Plus, I'm not authorized for overtime, and my shift ends soon. And my fiancée, Caroline, is making dinner for me."

"If this turns out to be something other than an accident, I know you'd want to make sure you covered all your bases," I advised.

McFalls put up his hands. "It's a tragedy, for sure, one of our own gone and all. A terrible accident. But that's it. Don't make a case where there is none."

I shook my head. "Can you at least bag and tag anything Ray could have touched? It won't take long. The EpiPen especially. I already told everyone not to touch it and leave it where it was."

McFalls looked at his phone. "I think it's unnecessary."

"But you'll take it and log it?" I pointed to the EpiPen lying on the floor next to Ray's body. Since I wasn't the cop on duty and I'd been a part of the poker game when Ray died, I knew I shouldn't handle it.

"Fine. Whatever." McFalls rubbed his neck. "But this is nothing more than an allergic reaction. It seems like you're trying too hard to make something out of it. Besides, I have enough open cases now, and this doesn't belong on my desk."

"I'm with McFalls," Howie put in. "Do what you gotta do. But in my opinion, you're trying to make something out of nothing. If I were you, I'd leave it alone."

"Howie, you know me better than that."

"And that's why I'm worried. I'm telling you as a friend, it was an accident, pure and simple," Howie declared.

Was Howie's resistance to my suggestion that McFalls look more into Ray's death due to his personal hatred of Ray, or was it something else?

"I'd listen to your pal," McFalls chimed in.

Howie let out a long breath. "José, any other time I'd be right there with you. You know that. But not this time. Sorry."

"Fine," I returned. "I'm going to stay awhile. See you later."

After patting me on the back, Howie left.

As I made my way to the poker table, I called my friend, Dr. Regina Fenny, at the coroner's office. "Can you do me a favor and come to Sanders' Tavern?"

"For a cold beer?" she asked.

"Maybe some other time."

"Ah, since it's not a social call, I assume you need me in a professional capacity."

I proceeded to get her up to speed on what had happened.

"I'll be there in five," she said, adding, "And José, since I'm doing you a favor and going to see your corpse, you owe me a few plus-ones."

CHAPTER 10

I approached Officer Nowak. "How are you holding up?"

"Okay, I guess, considering." Her eyes were red and swollen.

"I'm really sorry for your loss." That's what I said, but I could hear how detached and clichéd I sounded.

Nowak wept. "I'm numb. Like this is some weird nightmare."

"I'm sure." Again, I realized how weak that sounded. Even though I hadn't liked Ray, the dead deserved respect. I needed to muster some emotion while his niece was grieving.

"I can't believe that my uncle is dead. I just can't. He was more like a father to me than an uncle. My dad split when I was born, and Ray looked after my mom and me. He also protected us from my grandfather, who's a hard-ass to everyone. But mostly toward his two kids, my mom and Ray. It's a classic dysfunctional American family."

"Isn't everyone's family a little off in some way? I don't think there's any normal family, mine included. Families do the best they can with what they have," I added attempting to empathize with her.

"I guess so." She sniffed. "I'm glad that Uncle Ray stepped up after my dad left. He always had my back. He came to all of my softball and volleyball games, and he even helped support me through college. Now he's gone—" Nowak choked on her words. She wiped her swollen red eyes with the back of her hand.

I reached out and put a hand on her shoulder. "Let me know if there's anything I can do for you."

Nowak sniveled. "Thanks. I appreciate it."

"Would you like me to call any other family?" I offered.

"No, thank you." Nowak brushed hair from her eyes. "I'll do it. It's probably better coming from me anyway."

"José!" McFalls waved a plastic evidence bag holding the EpiPen. "You happy now?" He laid the bag on the bar top before walking over to Norman.

I gave him a thumbs-up, glad that he had followed through with my request.

Glancing around, I saw Patrice pick up Ray's cell phone from the floor. She began tapping on the screen. Why was she handling his phone? But first I had to turn to Nowak before she left. "Remember, the offer stands if you need anything, okay?"

Nowak's chest heaved as tears rolled down her face. She pulled out her phone.

I moved away from Nowak and asked the paramedics to wait a minute before they bagged and carried the body out. I intended my Medical Examiner friend to examine it first.

While I waited for Regina to arrive, I strode over to Patrice. "So, what are you doing with Ray's phone?"

Her eyes were wide as though I had startled her. Her voice went a pitch higher than normal. "I'm looking for his contacts. Someone needs to call his family."

"His niece, Officer Nowak, is doing that."

She clutched the phone in one hand. "Well, then, good. That's taken care of." She got up from the chair and pushed her glasses up the bridge of her nose. "This is unreal, isn't it?"

"Yes." I held out my hand. "And I'll take that from you."

"Why, of course." Patrice placed the phone in my palm. "It's really sad. I know he wasn't Mr. Popular and all. But Ray was very charming and sweet when he wanted to be."

That statement took me aback. Maybe she and Ray had been having an affair, after all. "Sweet and charming? Ray?"

"I mean, I've heard that about him." Patrice turned toward the front door.

Norman came up next to us. "Obviously, we need to call the tournament. Bag the chips, straighten things up, and call it a night."

"Hold off a second or two on cleaning up, okay?" I directed Norman.

Norman arched a brow. "What's going on?"

"Nothing."

"Gentlemen, it's been quite a night. I need to head home now." Patrice hugged us and then left.

Although I preferred everyone to stay put, I had no reason to keep any of them here. As of now, I had zero evidence this was anything more than an accident.

"Maggie looks like she's going to faint or something." Norman rubbed his chin. "Poor gal. I think we need to get someone to take her home."

I walked over to Bezu and Maggie by the bar. Maggie was seated on a barstool, her head hanging down. "Maggie, how are you doing?"

She placed a hand on her forehead as she squeezed her eyebrows together as though in pain. "I'm a bit lightheaded. But I'm okay." Her voice was soft and quiet. "I think I'll just go back home and lie down."

"I'd be glad to give you a ride. I'm all packed up and ready to go," Bezu offered. "It'll be my pleasure."

"No need. I have my moped." Maggie slid off the barstool and gathered her purse and sweater. She brushed her hair off her face. "Thank you for your concern. But really, I'm fine."

"Let me walk out with you, at least." Bezu gathered her basket and bag. Maggie and Bezu left as Regina entered.

"Hey there." Regina held her medical bag in one hand.

"Thanks for coming." I greeted her with a hug. "I know this isn't protocol, so I appreciate your indulgence."

"It comes with a price." She smiled. "Two boring weddings,

one drama-filled family gathering, and an eighties-themed birthday cookout."

We had known each other for several years now and had become good friends. Since we were both single, we were often each other's plus-one at events. She was one of the few people outside of Bezu, Annie Mae, Cat and my sisters who knew I was gay. Although she thought I was wrong not to live openly as a gay man, she honored my request for secrecy.

"One wedding. No family gathering. No eighties-themed cookout."

"No good." She held up one finger. "One wedding." Then she put another finger up. "One cookout. My final offer."

I shook her hand. "Deal."

I led her past Big Mike and Norman, who were at the bar talking, and Officer Nowak, who was on her cell phone. Regina greeted JJ and the paramedics.

McFalls strode over. "What's going on here?"

"I'd like Dr. Fenny to take a quick look at Ray," I explained.

"Did you get a call that I didn't?" McFalls asked. "'Cause the only call I got was that there was an officer down because of an allergic reaction. Don't make a case where it doesn't exist. This is not a homicide, José. The coroner's office will do a thorough review of the body and, I'm certain, determine that Ray's death was just a fluke. But if they think there's any foul play, which I highly doubt, I will follow through on it. I know what I'm doing. I don't need you on my back."

"Okay, fine." I had to tread lightly here and avoid overstepping my boundaries. "I just wanted a pal of mine, who *happens* to be the medical examiner, to take a quick look at Ray. Dickey said he read about a recall of EpiPens, and curiosity got the best of me is all."

"Since you're my friend, I'll look the other way this one time, but watch yourself. Okay?" Finished talking to me, he looked down at his phone.

"I understand. Thanks for cutting me some slack here," I told him.

Regina and I made our way over to Ray. We'd worked

together years ago in the crime lab. At one point I had seriously considered becoming a forensics scientist, but then I'd fallen in love with the complexities of explosives.

The paramedics were putting away their supplies. A body bag sat alongside the stretcher.

"I saw him inject himself in his left thigh," I told Regina.

She knelt down next to the body. After putting on disposable gloves, she began to inspect it. "He has all the signs of a severe allergic reaction. Swollen lips, eyelids. Large welts."

"Like I told you on the phone earlier, he was allergic to peanuts."

Taking out scissors, she cut the top left leg of his pants and then pulled back the fabric to reveal his skin. "Hmmm, this is unusual."

"What?" I squatted next to her.

"The site of the injection." She leaned in closer to Ray's exposed thigh. She shined a pen flashlight on one specific area. "There is massive swelling."

"I'm assuming that's not normal."

"No. Not normal at all."

"What does that mean?"

"I'm not sure." She peeled off her gloves. Her lips were formed in a tight line and her forehead creased.

"I can see by the look on your face that something is up."

"José, I've never seen this type of reaction at an EpiPen site. I can't say for certain what caused this until I get him on the table." She put her gloves and her penlight in her bag.

"Would you let me know as soon as you find out anything at all?" Together, we stood. "And would you mind putting a rush on it?"

She picked up her medical bag. "With Ray being a cop, I'm sure his autopsy will be a top priority. The whole force will be all over it."

"I'm sure it will be." But there was something bothering me about all of it that felt as though it needed to be taken care of immediately, as if it would be too late if we let it go. "Thanks for coming out tonight," I repeated.

"Get your tux ready; it's a formal wedding." She smiled. "And for the cookout, figure out which famous eighties person you'll be. I'm going as Madonna."

"I'll be the Invisible Man." I smiled.

"Wrong decade, smartass."

CHAPTER 11

"*Y*ou need to sit back a bit, Dad. All I see is your forehead," I said to the computer as I Skyped my family in Miami. I sat in my kitchen chair drinking coffee, wearing a T-shirt and crumpled boxer shorts. They only saw me from the waist up, so no need for real pants.

My black Labrador watchdog, J.K. Growling, and my gray cat, Meowly Cyrus, snuggled on a rug next to me near the kitchen table. My parents and I had already covered our typical weekly conversation basics—weather, health, gossip about relatives, and reports regarding which neighbor was annoying them.

"Dad, move back, here." My eldest sister, Juanita, put her hands on his shoulders and guided him back from the screen until his face was in full view. She leaned into the picture. "Better, José?"

"Much. Where did Mom go?"

My dad pointed to his side. "Right here."

I took in a deep breath, feeling exasperation. Juanita had the patience of a saint to deal with our elderly folks. "Juanita, can you please push the computer even further back so that I can see both of them?" If it weren't for my sister helping my folks Skype, this would have been an even worse disaster than it already was.

Mom put her mouth close to the screen as if she were talking into a phone. "So, anything new with you, son?"

"Mom, remember you just sit back here, normal. He'll be able to hear you just fine." Juanita rolled her eyes at me as if to say, *Aren't you lucky you don't have to deal with all of this?* "You'd think we haven't already done this a hundred times before," she said to my mom.

I smiled. "All is good here."

"Son, I'm not getting any younger. I hope during one of these Sky Pie computer face talks, you're going to tell me you've got a nice girl." Dad pointed a finger at the screen.

"It's Skype, not Sky Pie, honey." My mom leaned in front of him. She waved her hand at the screen as if shooing a fly. "Now, José, don't you worry. When it happens, it'll happen. Don't let him pressure you, baby. You have enough on your plate."

"What? It's so wrong to ask my *only son* if he's going to get married so he can give me a grandson to carry on the family name? I'm almost eighty years old; I can't wait forever." Dad looked indignant.

He was the typical Cuban macho man, the family patriarch who wanted all of us to have a life steeped in tradition. To him, this meant a heterosexual relationship where the man went to work and the woman stayed at home to have babies. My father griped but seemed to tolerate the fact that my sisters were college-educated career women and not housewives.

"You're so old-fashioned, Dad. What about your three daughters? Do we mean nothing to you?" Juanita shook her head.

"Never mind your father." Mom put her hand in front of Dad's face. "You do whatever you want in your own time, my precious baby boy."

"*Precious baby boy*? Really?" Juanita said.

"Of course you're *special*, too, my *sweet girl*." My mom patted Juanita's hand.

"I'm your *firstborn*. Of course I'm special." Juanita stuck her tongue at me.

"Real mature for a fifty-year-old." I smirked.

"I'm just saying, I'm not getting any younger, and I'd like to see you married and with a boy or two before I push up the daisies." Dad shook his finger at the screen.

"Yes, why aren't you married, José?" Juanita stuck her face close to the screen so that I could see her roll her eyes. She was coaxing me to come out to my parents. All my sisters knew I was gay and hated that I kept that secret from our folks. But they also knew how old-fashioned Dad was, so they went along with my request for secrecy.

I ignored both her and my father.

"All I ask you, José, is to find a nice girl. Settle down. And do it soon. At my age, I could go like that." My father snapped his fingers.

"Jeez, Dad, thanks for being so morbid at eight in the morning," Juanita scolded him.

I was grateful my eldest sister was there for my folks and seemed to have an unlimited supply of patience with them. Right now, I was at my limit.

I heard a knock at my front door and then the sound of it opening.

"Hello, José? It's Bezu. I'm so sorry to bother. But I need your help. I'm simply beside myself." Bezu's voice came from my hallway.

"Bezu, I'm back in the kitchen," I called.

My dog lifted one eyelid and then closed it as Bezu's footsteps came closer. So much for a watchdog. My cat didn't even move a whisker, but I didn't expect anything from her.

"Who are you talking to?" my mom asked.

"A friend of mine is at my house," I explained as Bezu entered the kitchen.

"José, I think I might have had something to do with killing Ray," Bezu blurted out.

I motioned to my open screen. "Bezu, these are my folks and my sister, Juanita."

Bezu's eyes went wide as she blushed and looked over my shoulder into the screen. "Have mercy." She took a breath as if to compose herself. "Good morning. So very nice to meet you, Mr.

and Mrs. Rodriguez, Juanita. I'm so sorry I'm interrupting you all."

"We Skype every Saturday morning, but trust me when I say that you did not interrupt anything. Actually, we were wrapping it up," I claimed hopefully.

"Did you say you think you *killed* someone?" my mom asked Bezu.

"Not on purpose, of course," Bezu told her, "but maybe accidentally."

"Oh, now this conversation is finally getting good. *Do tell*," Juanita said.

Bezu and I unfolded the events of the night before.

"So you see, Bezu had nothing to do with his death," I declared.

"Well, I'm not so sure about that," Bezu said before pausing. "What I haven't mentioned yet is that I think that I might have accidentally contaminated the food. Let me back up a second. I keep all of my oils under the sink, lined up next to each other."

"That's where I keep my oils, too," my mom added.

"Mom, we don't need to know where you keep your cooking stuff." Juanita rolled her eyes. "Bezu is in the middle of telling us her story."

"So far, I don't see a problem," I put in. "You knew not to use any peanut oil because of Ray's allergy."

"Well, yes, but…" Bezu paused. "While making the brownies, I used canola. Which is always the last bottle on the left." She sucked in a breath. "At least, *I thought I did*."

"*Thought* you did?" I repeated.

"Yes." Bezu continued, "Last night I tossed and turned, unable to quiet my mind, like I had a burr in my saddle. I couldn't settle down. I just kept second-guessing myself: did I use the wrong oil?"

"You think you used the peanut oil?" Juanita asked.

"Good question." My mother patted Juanita's arm.

"Maybe. I don't know." Bezu twisted her mouth.

"See? I'm as good at figuring things out as your *precious baby boy* is," Juanita asserted. "Go on, Bezu."

Bezu lowered her head. "So here I was, so meticulous about making sure there were no traces of any allergens, wearing gloves, sanitizing the counter and all. And now I fear I might have used the wrong oil."

"Wow. That is quite a mess if that's true." My dad shook his head.

"Yes, like she doesn't know that already, Captain Obvious," Juanita sighed.

"You need to show sympathy. This nice, pretty young lady is upset. We should leave them alone to figure this out," my mom decided.

"Yes, leave them alone. Don't they make a good-looking couple?" My dad smiled.

Bezu glared at me as if to say, *See, I told you not being honest about who you are will keep digging you deeper in lies.*

My mom rapped my dad on the arm. "Stop it."

My dad rubbed his arm. "Why did you hit me? Can't a dad want the best for his *only* son? I mean, if it turns out she's not a murderer, then they could get together."

Juanita circled her finger next to her head in the "he's crazy" motion.

Mom poked my dad in the side. "Enough. You're embarrassing them. You never mind him, Bezu. We'll see you in a few days, son. Let us know when your flight gets here, and we'll pick you up. Love you."

"I'll see you all soon. Love you." I closed the screen.

"Well, they are adorable." Bezu sat down.

"Adorably *annoying*."

CHAPTER 12

"*C*offee?" I offered Bezu as she sat with her head resting on her arms at my kitchen table. Digging in the sink, I found one almost-clean mug amongst a pile of dishes. Grabbing a paper towel, I wet it and then wiped the mug, afterward filling it with coffee.

"Did I fetch the wrong bottle of oil?" she mumbled. "I'm a horrible person who kills people with her food."

I set down a hot cup of coffee next to her and placed a hand on her back. "You had nothing to do with Ray's death."

Bezu lifted her head. "Of course I didn't plan to hurt anyone. I had nothing against him. I could never harm another human being."

"I know that."

"This is driving me crazy. The guilt. I think I have to file a report or something. I can't live with myself knowing that I might have, in some way, caused Ray's death." Bezu sipped her coffee. Her eyes welled up.

I leaned back against my kitchen counter. "You came here for my help, and here it is: *keep your mouth shut*. If your food had had anything to do with it, he would have reacted right after he ate it."

Bezu gave me a faint smile. As though she were trying to be

brave. "But what if it was such a minor amount in the food that it caused a slower response? Could that happen? Don't you think that I have to go into the station and let them know about the possible mix-up of oil? Please go with me, José. It's the right thing to do." Her eyes welled with tears.

I nodded, my heart feeling heavy for Bezu. I wanted to protect her like a brother would. "So I'll tell you again, and I want you to listen this time. Keep this to yourself. Ray's death was an *accident*."

Bezu sat back, wringing her hands. "José, this is the second time my food could be involved in killing someone."

"The other time, you were not the one who contaminated your food," I pointed out. "And you didn't do so this time, either."

"How else could he have been exposed? It must have been the food. *My food*. This is a whole mess of trouble." She sobbed. "The poor guy is dead because of me."

"Leave it alone." What if her food had contained the allergen? It would still be an accident, but Bezu would never be able to forgive herself.

She stood and pressed down the skirt of her sundress. "José, I just won't rest until I know for sure. I'm sick about this."

"Would it make you feel better if I did a little side investigation?"

"You would do that for me?"

I nodded.

"How? Can you analyze the food? Or find someone who could? What are you going to do?" She rested her delicate hand on my arm. "But you're on vacation. I don't want you to have to work."

"No big deal. Really. I have a few days before I leave for Miami."

"But what if you find out I somehow contributed to his death? Then what?" Her eyes welled up.

I cut her off. "We'll cross that bridge if we come to it. But I don't foresee a bridge."

∽

A FEW MINUTES AFTER BEZU LEFT, MY PHONE RANG.

"Is this a good time to talk?" Regina asked.

"Can I renegotiate? Just the wedding, no cookout," I tried. The thought of dressing up as an eighties idol made me cringe. Since my suggestion about going as the Invisible Man was off the table, I supposed I could go as Eric Estrada from the TV show *CHiPs*. That would be pretty easy: he was Cuban and a cop. Not too much of a stretch and no need for a costume.

"It's a done deal. No takebacks. I wanted to let you know that I have some preliminary results from Ray's autopsy."

"And?"

"Well…" She hesitated. "There are anomalous aspects at the injection site. It doesn't show the response one would expect."

I let out a long breath. "Do you know why he had an atypical response?"

There was a long pause. "Not yet. I'm sending tissues to pathology. I need to see the EpiPen, and that's the problem."

"What?" I asked.

"The EpiPen is not with the logged-in evidence."

"It's not?" My gut tightened. What had McFalls done with it?

"Nope."

"Let me look into it. I'll get back to you on that."

"The sooner the better."

"You know something, don't you?"

"Not on the record."

"Okay. How about off the record?"

She paused again but ended up explaining. "I know the injection site was swollen, and that isn't normal. I can only speculate what might have caused it. Maybe Ray had peanuts on the hand he used to inject himself, or maybe the pen was faulty, or—well, it could be a myriad of things. Without the pen, I have no way of knowing for sure."

"Could foul play be involved?"

"Hard to say. But the anomaly at the injection site does

concern me. However, I can't conclude homicide without further information."

"Is there any way that the medicine itself caused that reaction?" I asked.

"No, I've never heard of that." Regina cleared her throat. "And the autopsy results indicate there was no epinephrine in his system."

"Wait? And you're just telling me this now? Why didn't you lead with that? That's huge." I felt a rush of adrenaline. "Then Dickey could be right. It might be product malfunction."

"That's one conclusion. As of now, though, I have no choice but to categorize it as an accidental death. If you want a more definitive answer, get me the EpiPen, and I'll go from there."

"Got it." I took a deep breath. "This is important to me."

"But you weren't friends."

"It's personal."

"Like how *personal?*"

"Sorry, Regina. I'm trying to help a friend, so right now I can't go into any details. Trust me on this."

"You know I do."

Truly grateful, I added, "I really appreciate your help."

"We'll talk soon."

"I owe you," I admitted.

"I'll add it to your tab. Maybe I'll get you to come to the boring drama filled family party, after all." She laughed and ended the call.

I tried out a theory that pinged around my head. If Bezu had accidentally contaminated the food with peanut oil, which had then caused a severe allergic in Ray, who'd then used his EpiPen to stop the reaction, which had then malfunctioned—the whole thing could simply have been an epic catastrophe of misfortunes.

Then again, that was only one theory.

And I was concerned about the swelling. The first step in the puzzle was to find the EpiPen.

CHAPTER 13

The next morning, I walked into the precinct wearing khaki shorts, flip-flops, and a Hawaiian shirt.

"You look busy." I approached McFalls, who sat at a desk over a pile of papers.

"What are you doing here? Aren't you off for the next week or so?" McFalls eyed me. "You look like a beach bum," he said and laughed.

"You're hilarious." I glanced around the room. A few officers stood at the back. "I came to see you."

McFalls leaned back in his chair. "So, what's up?"

"I couldn't leave on vacation right away because I missed the pervasive smell of disinfectant and coffee." I plopped into the empty chair next to his desk. "With a slight hint of old books."

"Even the air fresheners can't hide the smell. It's a permanent part of the building. Some call it ambiance others call it offense."

I smiled. "No kidding."

McFalls crossed his arms. "So, why are you really here?"

I wanted to tread lightly. After all, he'd looked the other way when I'd asked the ME to examine Ray's body at Sanders' Tavern. "I wanted to find out what's going on with Ray's case."

McFalls let out a loud breath. "*Case*? It was an accident. A super tragic one. But an accident all the same. There is no case."

"That's open for discussion, right? I mean, don't we need to look at all the evidence?"

McFalls brows furrowed. "Evidence? What evidence?"

"The EpiPen."

McFalls looked away from me. "Oh, yeah. It was supposed to be logged in last night."

"I just spoke to the ME, and she said it wasn't."

"I bet those clowns down in evidence still haven't gotten to it yet." McFalls opened a drawer in his desk and pulled out a stack of papers.

"Let me get this straight. You bagged the pen, right?"

"Yeah, I held it up and showed you. Don't you remember?"

Of course, I did, but I was trying to get all the facts correct. "Yeah. I saw you set it on the bar top. What happened next?"

McFalls glared at me. "Are you interrogating me?"

"No, I just want to know where it is."

McFalls picked up a pen and scribbled something on a piece of paper. "I assumed it was logged in. It's not my problem the nimrods in evidence don't have it. José, can you back off with all the questions and just go and enjoy your time off?"

"I'm trying to." I rubbed the bridge of my nose. He didn't make eye contact with me, I took that as a sign he was not being sincere. "But I'm also trying to find a vanishing item."

"To be clear here," McFalls asserted still not looking at me, "even if you find the EpiPen, there's no case. It was a clear-cut accident."

If it wasn't in the evidence room, then maybe he'd lost it? Or left it in his car or at the bar? Right now, it seemed like he was trying to protect his reputation with his soon-to-be chief of police father-in-law.

"We all had a rough night, José. I know that everyone was drinking at the poker game, including you. You might be thinking that more went on last night than really happened. I get it. Cop brain is always on. But last night was nothing more than a tragedy."

"Just to make sure you know, I only had two beers, and my thoughts were crystal-clear." I could feel my patience wearing thin. "And my drinking is inconsequential to the EpiPen being MIA."

"Listen, I'm not your enemy. We're on the same team. Ray died of a severe allergic reaction. *Non-case* closed."

"Dickey mentioned a recall on faulty injectors. Ray might have used a defective one. We won't know unless we see it."

"You've got the TV lawyer on this?"

"He gave his business card to Ray's niece."

"Nowak?"

I nodded. "Knowing Dickey, I bet he already represents the family."

"Jeez." McFalls ran a hand through his hair. "Damn ambulance chaser. Last night I had two missed calls, one from the ME and one from Dickey. But if it's a product liability case, then that's not a crime."

"Still, if it is a product liability case, we don't have the product. That's the problem."

"José, you and I have known each other for a long time, and you know I earned my position."

"Yeah, that's not in question." Although what *was* in question was his story and attitude. Right now, he was acting like a grade-A jerk.

"Listen, my team did their job last night. They did everything by the book, dotted the i's and crossed the t's. We've got it covered. You don't need to worry about it. And I've got a lot going on already." He stood.

I followed suit, standing next to his desk. "We all do." I wondered why McFalls was not feeling protective of a fellow cop. Was he afraid that if anything went wrong with his handling of Ray's death it would reflect poorly on him? Or did he hate Ray enough not to care about him?

I also suspected that he might not have ever taken the evidence from the bar. Or if he did take it from the bar, he left it in his car or lost it. What I knew for sure was that my buddy in the evidence room was not a nimrod as McFalls claimed, and he wouldn't have lost evidence. My gut said that the injector never made it to the police station. I just needed McFalls to admit it.

"To make sure I understand, the EpiPen made it here, right?"

"We already went over this. And you of all people should know that we don't need to be chasing our tails on stupid stuff. And we definitely don't need to add any more to our already stacked workload, right? I've got this covered. Trust me, none of us here are taking Ray's death lightly." McFalls waved his hand. "Get out of here. And have a great vacation."

~

"Thanks. I appreciate it." I hung up the call with the precinct evidence room. They had no record of anything turned in from McFalls during the past twenty-four hours.

There was no doubt in my mind that McFalls was trying to cover his ass. He'd deliberately lied to me. I walked out of the precinct and was immediately assaulted by the pungent smell of the hot, humid air, quite a change from yesterday's cold snap.

A car pulled up one over from mine in the parking lot. Nowak got out. "Sergeant Rodriguez, can I talk to you?"

"Hey, Nowak, how you holding up?" I held my key and fobbed my car door to unlock.

Nowak covered her eyes from the sun's glare as she approached me. "Okay, I guess. I miss him so badly. I'm so shocked. I've never cried so much in my life."

"I'm really sorry. Remember, if there's anything I can do for you, let me know."

"Actually—" She hesitated. "There is."

"What do you need?"

"My grandfather and my mom appointed me to handle the issues involved in Ray's death. I need to find out if the shot could've been defective."

"You've been talking to Dickey, then?"

She nodded. "He thinks this could be a product liability case. I mean, once we get the forensics on it."

"Even if the device was faulty, you can't use it in court. It wouldn't be admissible."

"Why?"

"Because it's missing." I crossed my arms over my chest.

"But I saw him bag it up last night."

"I did too. But apparently that's as far as it got. I don't know what to tell you." Feeling tightness in my neck, I rolled my head to try to loosen up. "It's probably sitting in McFalls' car. Or left at the tavern. Hell, it could've been thrown away, for all I know. He ducked any direct questions I asked. I think he screwed up and was hoping no one would notice."

Nowak's shoulders slumped. "So, the chain of custody is broken. Anyone could have tampered with it."

Her disappointment was second only to my suspicions. I nodded. "The case, if there even is one, is already compromised. Considering it's civil evidence and not criminal evidence, maybe Dickey could still work his magic on it, but I'm not sure."

"I still want it. I need to know." Her voice went quiet as she sniffed. Nowak shoved her hands in her pockets.

A load rumble of a motorcycle went past. When I glanced toward the sound, I briefly stared at a handsome guy walking near the chain-link fence.

Nowak commented, "You know him?"

Ashamed that she'd noticed, I felt heat rise in my chest.

I decided to ignore her comment and continued the conversation where we had left off. "I'd like to know what really happened to your uncle, too." I wondered if Ray's family could sue McFalls and the police department for losing the EpiPen. Since there was no private right of action against a public entity like the police, it wouldn't go anywhere, but it would result in a whole lot of bad press. Even without that, I was sure the press would have a field day exploiting McFalls' incompetence. "I'd like to help you, but my hands are tied."

"Maybe. Maybe not." Nowak glanced at me and over at the set of parked cars. "That's McFalls' car over there, right?"

I nodded.

Nowak ran over to her own car. She popped open her trunk and extracted a slim jim lockout tool.

"Hey. Don't wanna see you do something stupid, kid," I called to her.

"Then don't look." Nowak made her way over to McFalls' vehicle.

For God's sake. I should just walk away. Get in my car and forget about this idiot. Instead, I followed her.

Nowak slid the lock pick in the passenger-side window. I watched nervously and scanned the area to make sure no one saw her. A group of officers milled about near the far end of the lot, but they were chatting amongst themselves and paying us no mind.

After a few tries, Nowak threw the slim jim on the ground and went to the base of a nearby tree to pick up a rock the size of an orange.

"Whoa. Wait a minute." I grabbed the rock from her hand. "What the hell are you doing?"

"I've gotta get in."

"You don't even know if anything's in there."

"But it might be. If he bagged it, and it's not logged in, then it's probably in his car, right? I have to know." Her words faltered and choked in her throat as she began to cry.

"Fine." Letting out a groan, I threw down the rock. "Just sit tight."

I picked the thin metal strip off the ground. After glancing around and seeing nobody, I shimmied it in the window. One second later, I had the door unlocked. I turned to Nowak with a smile. "And that, Officer Nowak, is how it's done." I opened the door and pressed the master unlock button. "You check the backseat."

I rummaged through the pile of empty fast-food wrappers and coffee cups. There was a stack of wedding invitation samples and a pair of running shoes, but no EpiPen. "Any luck back there?"

"Nothing. I'll check the trunk," Nowak offered.

I poked my head up. It was only a matter of time before someone would be in the lot.

I walked back to Nowak. "Anything?"

She sighed. "Nothing but jumper cables, a spare tire, and

junk. So, no. But we gotta keep looking. It's gotta be here some-where. It has to be."

"But it's not."

"Do you think it's still at the bar?"

"Maybe. Maybe not." I knew I'd go over to the bar next. Tension settled in my upper body, and I rolled my shoulders back. "We're done here."

"I don't want to give up. I can't. I just can't." She closed the trunk.

"But we have to."

"Maybe you have to quit. But I don't have to. This is about my uncle's death."

"I get it. But can you trust me on this?" I knew I was going to pursue my search for the EpiPen. "It'll work out. You'll get answers about what happened to your uncle. Maybe not right now, right here, but you will."

"Can you promise me that?" she wanted to know.

"You have my word on it."

"Fine. I heard you're a man of your word." She nodded. "You know, we make a great team."

"There is no *we*." I pressed the lock-all button and shut the door. "If anyone asks, you know nothing about this."

"Got it."

She grabbed the slim jim and went to her car.

As I neared my vehicle around the corner, I heard my name called out. It startled me and made my heart jump a beat.

"José, I thought you'd be gone by now." McFalls walked up next to me.

Had he seen me digging through his car earlier?

I stopped and thumbed toward my car. "I'm leaving now."

"Good. I'm heading to look at wedding venues. If it were up to me, we'd just go to the justice of peace and be done with it."

"I bet." I smiled.

"Have a good vacation. I heard you're going to Miami to visit your family."

"I leave in a few days."

"Good." McFalls stopped and then waved a hand. "Oh, and did you hear a car was broken into here last night? You'd think that a precinct parking lot would be the safest place in the city."

I grinned. "You'd think so."

CHAPTER 14

*A*fter leaving the precinct, I went back to my house. I needed to concentrate a bit on mundane tasks like cleaning and laundry to clear my head. I shoved dishes in the dishwasher and turned it on. Taking a stack of newspapers, I piled them on my back deck for recycling. My overflowing laundry basket needed attention, so I started a load.

When my house looked somewhat decent again, J.K. Growling and I took a walk in Forsyth Park. All the while, I thought of what I could do about the whole EpiPen debacle. I couldn't let it go. The EpiPen and the autopsy results were both critical in finding out what happened to Ray. Hopefully, the EpiPen had been faulty and that had caused Ray's death, so... case closed.

I remembered well the promise I'd made to Nowak and Bezu to find out what had happened to Ray. I always kept my agreements.

My phone rang, and I absent-mindedly hit answer.

"You said if there was anything you could do, to ask you," Nowak said.

Something told me I'd regret making that offer. "Sure. What can I do for you?"

"Since we didn't find the EpiPen in McFalls' car, I have to keep looking. That's where you come in. Please help me find it."

"No way." Even though I had planned to look for it myself, I didn't want her involved.

"Please. I know my uncle was a bit of a jerk to you. I'm sorry for that. But he was my *uncle*. He was really *good* to me." She sounded smaller with each word. "I can't walk away without knowing what really happened. Plus, the police therapist I saw this morning says I need closure."

"Listen, I know this is really a hard time for you and you're grieving." I paused for a moment. "Just give yourself some time. As far as the injector, it's best to move on and let that go. The ME's calling it accidental death."

Nowak was silent for a second. "I won't let it go until I know for sure."

"I get it. But you might not have a choice in the matter." I was still trying to avoid telling her that I planned on finding the injector myself. She should not be involved. For one thing, if she did find the shot, it might ruin her family's chances of getting a settlement from the EpiPen manufacturer, who could claim she might have tampered with it to swing the case in her monetary favor.

"But, it's not *right*. Nothing about what happened to my uncle feels *right*. How did he get exposed to peanuts in the first place? And then why didn't the shot work?"

Those were the very same questions I'd been mulling over. "I don't know."

"Pardon me, Sergeant, I'm not trying to be insubordinate by saying what I'm about to say. But the tone of your voice suggests that you don't want to leave this alone any more than I do."

"You're way off base, Nowak." I tried to sound convincing. I didn't want her involved in my off-the-record investigation. "I can't help you. And I suggest you leave it alone."

It was hard to sound believable when all I could think about was how wrong all of this felt. I certainly didn't plan to leave it alone.

~

Upon entering Sanders' Tavern, I flicked on the lights and then locked the front door behind me. Norman had given me the entry code so I could go look around before the place opened that afternoon. The poker table used for the tournament was gone. From the smell of Pine-Sol and the neat lineup of chairs along the bar, it looked like the place had been cleaned. Which meant that I might be wasting my time searching for anything.

As I walked around, I scanned the area. I started my search with the most obvious place, the floor. I bent down and checked under the bar in case someone had kicked the injector under it. I explored everywhere the EpiPen might have skidded during the effort to save Ray. When that produced nothing other than dirty hands and knees, I moved to the bar. I checked every shelf, drawer, sink, and container. I still came up empty.

Then I made my way to the area near the back door next to the restrooms.

In the back corner of the room stood a large trash can that looked as though it hadn't been emptied in a while. Digging through trash hadn't been on my list of things to do today. But I could hear my dad's voice loud and clear. *Why do a job at all if you aren't planning on doing it right?*

I'm not sure dumpster diving is what he had in mind for that life lesson, but the principle held true. I stepped over to the can and began pulling out the contents. After emptying everything onto the floor, I felt confident that the shot was not in there, so I put everything back in the can.

A loud bang sounded from outside the back door, only a few inches from where I stood. Then I heard scratching sounds on the metal, followed by more banging. The door handle rattled up and down.

Someone was trying to break into the tavern.

I put one hand over my gun and the other hand on the door-knob. I could feel my heart pounding as adrenaline pumped in my veins.

Drawing my gun, I swung open the door. "Freeze!" I yelled.

Nowak stood outside the door, a crowbar in one of her upheld hands.

"What are you doing here?" I holstered my gun. "I could've shot you."

"I didn't know anyone was here." Nowak lowered her shaking arms. "I wanted to do some investigating."

"By breaking and entering?"

"Well, um…"

"Breaking the law seems to be a habit of yours." I grunted. "I think you're in the wrong profession."

"Sergeant, if I'm not mistaken, *you* were the one who broke into McFalls' car. Isn't that right?"

"Only because you were going to put a rock through his window." I took a long, deep breath and squeezed the bridge of my nose. "Didn't I just tell you to leave this alone? Go home, Nowak." I went inside the bar.

Nowak followed me in. "Then why aren't you leaving it alone?"

"None of your business." I locked the back door.

When I turned, I saw Nowak going through the trashcan. She wasn't giving up. Stubborn, just like Juanita. I had to laugh.

"It's not in there," I told her.

"I knew it!" Nowak looked up with a handful of trash and grinned.

"You know nothing." The kid had me. But darned if I'd admit that.

Nowak put the trash back. "You and I are looking for the same thing. We don't have to double our efforts; we can work together." She thrust out her hand for me to shake.

I stuck my hands in my pockets.

She locked eyes with me. "I'm going to do this with or without your help."

At least if I was with her, I could stop her from doing something stupid. I moved past her outstretched hand. "Fine."

"Really?" She sounded excited.

"Don't make me regret it." I walked to the front door.

She followed on my heels like an eager puppy. "I promise I won't break any more laws, *unless I need to*."

"There you go: you just busted your agreement."

As I locked up the door, I noticed her standing beside me, her eyes wide with anticipation.

"Sergeant, what next?"

I had to figure out how to keep her involved without getting her in trouble. "How about you go over the list of people who were at the poker game last night? Maybe one of them saw the injector. Let's start with that."

"Thank you for giving me a chance. It's not easy being a female cop, you know. I feel like I have to work twice as hard to prove myself."

I huffed. She had no idea what hardships and discrimination were. "Then work hard, prove yourself."

"You have no idea," she mumbled as she walked behind me to my car

"No. I don't know what it's like being a female. But I do know about being a minority in a system rigged against you."

"Oh?"

I unlocked my car and turned to her. "My parents were immigrants. They came to Miami from Cuba and knew little English. My dad worked the hot, dirty grunt jobs no one else wanted. Lawn maintenance and landscaping. Trying to support my mom and his four children, he worked long hours for little pay, if he got paid at all."

"Why would he work without pay?"

How much should I tell her so that she'd know I understood and would show her no special treatment? "Never mind."

"But you brought it up. Now I want to know."

She was persistent, and she was right. I had brought it up, and I should tell her. I rested against the side of my car. "My dad worked as a day laborer under a boss who decided that it was optional to pay his non-English-speaking employees."

Nowak leaned against my car. "That's horrible. How did the boss get away with that?"

"Most of his workers weren't citizens, and they didn't speak the language. He knew that they had no rights and were grateful when they got paid at all." I tensed up as I thought about this time in my life. My stomach compressed and heat rose in my chest.

"But someone should have stuck up for them."

My heart raced as I remembered. "I finally did. I was eighteen and tall for my age. I heard my mom crying that we had no money for groceries *again* because Dad's boss had refused to pay him. This happened so many times that right then and there, I'd had enough. I went to the foreman's office, and let's just say that after that, my dad and the others were paid what they were owed."

"Wow. You stuck up for him when he couldn't stick up for himself." She locked eyes with me. "Is that why you became a cop?"

Actually, it was. But I had to get our relationship back on a professional level. "Sit tight until you hear from me." I got in my car.

"You got it, partner," she agreed.

I looked at her.

"I meant, Sergeant, sir," she added.

I smiled to myself as I started the car and drove away. Hopefully, this would be a successful mentorship and not a disaster. I had no desire to get both of us fired.

CHAPTER 15

*a*fter I grabbed something to eat, I passed by Sanders' Tavern, saw Norman's car out front, and stopped in. I had to find out if he had seen the EpiPen.

"Thanks for letting me look around this morning," I told Norman.

Big Mike was slicing limes behind the bar. Norman sat at the counter with a stack of papers in front of him.

"Glad to help. Did you find what you were looking for?" Norman asked.

"No." I sat on barstool next to him. "Did either one of you happen to see the EpiPen after Ray collapsed?"

"Not me." Norman shook his head over his paperwork.

"The shot thing?" Big Mike looked up from slicing. "Yeah. Matter of fact, I did."

"Where was it?" I asked.

He pointed to a far corner of the bar. "It was in a plastic bag sitting over there."

"Do you remember what time you saw it there?"

"Might have been around the time the paramedics were still here. I can't remember for sure." Big Mike set down his knife on the cutting board.

"Did you see who put it there?"

"That detective that came, McFalls, I think." Mike filled a glass with ice water and handed it to me.

"Thanks." I took a drink. "Do you happen to know what happened to it?"

"No. I just assumed McFalls took it because one minute it was there, then I turned around to wash some bar glasses, and it was gone." Big Mike thumbed behind him.

"But you didn't see him take it?"

"No."

"Maybe it fell or got swept into the trash," I suggested.

Mike shook his head. "I'm the one who dealt with the trash and mopped up. I'm pretty sure I would've seen it. Maybe someone took it."

"Did you see anyone near the bar at that time? Standing around or walking toward it?" I asked.

"No. Then again, things got pretty crazy with all that was happening."

"Can you think of anything else from last night that felt *off* to you?"

"Besides a guy dying?" He laughed. "Sorry, I didn't mean to be rude. Even though I hated the guy, it was a horrible thing that happened to him."

I nodded, struggling to put the puzzle pieces together. The pen had definitely been bagged, but it was no longer at the bar. McFalls said he took it and logged it into evidence but that doesn't ring true at all.

"So, why you so interested in all of this? I heard it was just an accident," Big Mike said.

"It very well may be. But Dickey thinks it could've been a defective device, and that might have contributed to Ray's death."

Big Mike shook his head. "That would suck if it was meant to save his life and killed him instead."

"No kidding." I rubbed my temples. "But we won't know for sure until we get a hold of it. And right now it seems to have vanished into thin air."

Norman spoke up. "You know, Dickey has been bugging me

about that damned thing, too. You'd think it was the Holy Grail the way everyone's talking about it."

I chuckled at Norman's analogy. My thoughts returned to the mystery. If I was right and McFalls never took it after he bagged it, that meant someone in the room must have taken it. But why, and who? I needed to know, but without an actual police investigation, I couldn't exactly interrogate everyone who had access. Then again, I might not have to.

"Sorry I couldn't be of more help." Big Mike said.

"I'm not much help, either," Norman added as he set a piece of paper down.

I decided to run with my idea. "What do you think about finishing the tournament tonight, Norman?" I felt like a complete ass for even asking, considering what had happened.

"Are you serious?" Norman glared at me. "That's pretty cold."

I cringed, knowing how the request made me look, but I had to have everyone back together. The sooner the better, so that people's memories were still fresh. "I think Ray would've wanted us to carry on without him."

"Oh, you do? Now that he's dead, you're suddenly his friend speaking on his behalf?" Norman grinned.

"He's a cop. Cops stick up for each other." It was the best explanation I could muster.

"Okay, I get it. I'll give everyone a call. Tell them we're finishing the tournament." Norman stacked his papers. "What about Ray's spot?"

"What if his niece, Nowak, took his place?" I suggested.

"Hmmm." Norman stood. "When I'm making calls, I'll run that past the others. I'll give them the option of continuing the game for a chance to win the big kitty or refunding their buy-in and entry fee. It's got to be unanimous. Trust me, though, they'll all be in favor of playing."

"How do you know that they'll all agree?"

"People are greedy. A chance to win five thousand is much more attractive than getting a refund."

"I'll see you later this evening."

∿

CALLS TO BOTH PARAMEDICS LED ME NOWHERE. NEITHER ONE OF them had taken the EpiPen nor seen anyone else taking it.

Back home, I threw the wet clothes from the wash into the dyer.

My cell rang, and I picked up.

"This is embarrassing for me, but I feel that I have to explain myself," McFalls said.

"Okay shoot."

"I hated misleading you. I did bag the EpiPen and then I set it on the bar. I told one of the officers there that night to grab it and log it in. I assumed they had when I saw it was gone."

"Let me guess, they didn't?"

"After you came in this morning, I knew I'd dropped the ball and couldn't explain why it wasn't in the evidence room."

"Yeah, you threw my buddy under the bus calling him a nimrod," I added.

"Sorry about that, you put me in the spot. It was the first I'd heard that it wasn't logged in. I had to come up with some sort of explanation until I could figure out what happened myself. I know that I have to take responsibility for what happened, but when you came in asking a bunch of questions, I had no answers for you then."

"So that's why you avoided my questions."

"Yes." He paused. "After you left this morning, I talked to the officer on my team. He said when he went back to get the bag I'd left on the bar, it wasn't there. He thought I must have grabbed it."

I let out a long breath. "You both assumed the other took it and logged it in."

"Yes, that appears to be the case. I've sent someone over to Sanders Tavern to look for it now. Maybe it fell on the floor, or was accidently thrown away."

"Suit yourself. But you're not going to find it. I was just there."

"Jeez. This is a mess."

"I'm trying to help you here, but you've got to be honest with me moving forward."

"Jose, I'll take the blame on this. You can let me handle the missing shot, I'll take care of it."

"Did you ever think that someone there last night took it?"

"Maybe." He huffed. "I'll look into it, you don't have to worry about it."

"I don't know why I'd worry, I mean it's not like there was evidence lost or anything."

"I deserved that. But can we start fresh, and trust that I'm taking care of this?"

"I gotta go." I intentionally dodged his question. Turnaround is fair play. I clicked off.

I called Nowak.

"So, what next?" Nowak asked.

I got her up to speed on what I had found out. Or, in this case, what I hadn't found out. "But I'll see everyone tonight at Sanders' Tavern. That'll be a good time for me to poke around and find out if anyone saw the device. Hopefully find out who has it."

"You think someone might have taken it?"

"Yes. Big Mike said he saw the pen at one point last night. I searched the bar, and it wasn't there. It didn't get thrown away or fall on the floor. McFalls doesn't have it, and it's not logged in the evidence room. *Something is up*. I don't think it's an accident. One of the people at the tournament must've deliberately taken it."

"Why would they?" she asked.

"Good question." And I wanted to know the answer.

"If someone did take it, they must have been trying to cover up something. But what?" Nowak asked.

She was pretty sharp. "That's the million-dollar question."

"This changes everything. You're right—the only people who could have taken it were there last night," Nowak said.

"That's why I asked Norman to continue the tournament. We need to have everyone together again. Then we can try to get answers to some things that aren't making sense," I said.

"Now I can't help thinking that this might be way more than a possible product malfunction." Her voice was low and soft.

"One step at a time. Don't jump to conclusions. We don't have any facts yet." I paused. "Can you play poker?"

"Yeah. I learned from Uncle Ray. I can hold my own."

"Then you're taking his place tonight."

"Good." She paused. "Since I'll be there, I can help you with interrogations."

"We are not *interrogating* anyone."

"Right. Got it." Her voice vacillated as though she was winking as she spoke.

"I mean it. Why don't you just let me handle the investigation?"

"But we already agreed we'd work together. So, I'll see you tonight. And I'll think of questions to ask everyone, okay?"

"If I said no, then what?"

"I'd tell you I'm still doing what I want."

"That's not what I want to hear." I hung up.

CHAPTER 16

That evening when I walked in the tavern, Bezu was setting up a buffet on the bar top.

I hugged her. "How are you doing?"

"I'm fine. I had reservations about doing the meal, what with everyone's allergies and all and what happened to Ray that may or may not have been my fault. But I had to get back on the horse, so to speak."

"I'm glad you're here." Behind me, in the back corner of the room, everyone was at the table. I was the last to arrive.

"But I have to admit, I was really surprised that Norman asked me to come tonight. It seems rather insensitive to continue the game, considering what happened."

Inside, my stomach turned. What I was about to say would sound cold-hearted, so I hesitated. "I'm the one who suggested it."

Bezu set down her basket. "José, I'm shocked. I know he was a horse's backside to you, but still. The poor guy died."

"Yeah, well. We had to continue sooner or later. There's still five thousand in the pot. And no one wanted a refund on his or her buy-in or entry fee. Tonight's as good as any other." I avoided her stare.

Bezu touched my arm. "I know you too well. You're onto something."

To change the subject, I looked over at her spread of sweets, chicken fingers, and chips. "The food smells great."

"Avoiding the question, huh? That's fine." She straightened a pile of napkins next to the plate of brownies. "Did you find out how Ray got exposed to the peanuts last night?"

"Not yet. But I'm working on it."

"I figured that's why everyone was here."

I looked away and nodded.

She let out a long sigh. "I wonder if I should have everyone sign a release form before they eat my food from now on."

"No need. I can almost guarantee Ray's death had nothing at all to do with your food." Hoping beyond belief that this statement was true, I added, "I'll find out for sure what happened. Trust me."

"I know you will. Thank you. I can't rest until I'm one hundred percent sure it wasn't my fault."

I nodded. "Listen, I have to go back to the table."

Big Mike was behind the bar.

Maggie shuffled and fanned the cards. Everyone was in their same seat around the table. Nowak stood nearby, chatting with Norman.

I said hi to everyone. Then I turned to Nowak. "Can I talk to you for a second?"

Nowak and I moved out of earshot of the group. "Remember, sit in the corner and keep quiet."

"Real funny, Sergeant. There is no corner." She winked. "And even so, *nobody puts baby in a corner*."

Her quote from *Dirty Dancing* made me roll my eyes. "You know what I mean." I was just about to lay down the rules for what she should and should not do as far as questioning when Norman called out to us.

"It's time to play," he told us.

Nowak smiled. "Trust me, I've got this. *Partner*."

I let out a short groan.

We walked back to the table. Patrice motioned for Nowak to take Ray's chair.

"I'm so sorry about your uncle." Patrice reached over and put her hand on top of Nowak's. "I heard they gave you bereavement leave for several days, and I'm so glad they did. You're mighty brave to be sitting in for your uncle tonight after what happened to him."

"I'm playing this game in his honor. If I win, I think I'll use the money to start a college scholarship fund in his name," Nowak told her.

"Oh. Good idea," Patrice replied. "Making the best of a very sad situation. Please let me know if there's anything I can do for you."

JJ put in his two cents. "I keep going over what happened last night, and I still can't wrap my head around it. One minute he was there and the next, gone. I'm really sorry, Nowak."

"It's a tragedy for sure," Howie added.

Big Mike and Norman also expressed their sympathies.

"Kid, I hate what happened. But now that you've got me on your side, I'll make sure that your uncle didn't die in vain." Dickey waved his hand at Big Mike. "Two scotch and Cokes on the rocks."

Big Mike took everyone's drink order. While we waited for Maggie to finish shuffling, Norman and Nowak had a side conversation. Howie, sitting to my left, turned to me. "You know, I totally wanted to suggest continuing the tournament, but I didn't want to sound like a jerk."

"I thought it was pretty callous, too," Patrice added.

"I mean, I'd rather have a chance at five K than just get my money back," Dickey put in. "But truth be told, continuing the game so soon is a tad bit heartless."

"I agree." JJ leaned in. "Thanks for being the jerk for us, José."

I felt heat rise in my chest. Being a jerk was not who I was. I ignored the remarks. Having them think I was a snake was a small price to pay if I could prove Ray's death was not an accident. I had to concentrate on the real reason I was here.

Maggie dealt the cards.

As we played, we engaged in the usual small talk. When I felt the timing was right, I led the conversation to a place where I could ask the necessary questions. "Feels weird without Ray here, doesn't it?"

Everyone nodded.

"He was way too young to die, that's for sure. If it weren't for that damned device not working, I bet he'd still be here." Dickey tapped the top of his cards.

"You know for sure the shot was defective?" JJ asked. "Sorry, Nowak, I don't want to seem insensitive talking about your uncle's death."

"No harm." Nowak glanced at me, her eyes welling up.

Clearly, this was rough for her.

She sucked in a deep breath and then blew it out. "It's okay. I want to talk about him."

Good job. She'd composed herself and was helping move the conversation in the direction I needed. "Only problem is that we don't know where the EpiPen is. It seems to have vanished into thin air. Did anyone here happen to see it?" I asked.

"Not me. I doubt anyone was paying it much attention." Patrice bit her bottom lip as she studied her cards.

"I saw McFalls bag it, but that was it," Howie said.

"It's not like that was the focus of the night." JJ shrugged his shoulders.

"I'm almost positive Ray died because of a faulty product." Dickey guzzled his drink.

"But, we don't know that for sure," I insisted.

"Yeah, no kidding. Without the EpiPen, we have no way of proving anything." Dickey sighed. "And Ray's family won't be able to seek compensation for his death." He looked over at Nowak.

Nowak sighed, too. "I don't care about the money. It's about making a company take responsibility for what they did and making sure that it doesn't happen to anyone else."

"But I could get you a lot of money if we could find that damned thing." Dickey huffed. "Too bad it's MIA."

I looked at my hand of cards, although I found it difficult to concentrate. Who had taken the EpiPen, and why?

"It couldn't have just disappeared." Nowak glanced at every-one. "One of you *must* know where it went."

Her neck was red, and she sat at the edge of her seat.

I sensed her irritation and impatience. I needed to head her off before she said something stupid. I caught her eye and gave her a look that said, *I got this.*

Most of all, I didn't appreciate her accusatory tone. I needed to soften her statement and do some damage control. "Nowak, we know that you're under a lot of stress with what happened to your uncle. And we're all really sorry about that. I'm sure if anyone here could help you out, they would."

"Why would anyone here want the damn thing?" Howie questioned.

"I agree," JJ added.

"No one would." Patrice looked at Nowak.

"Well, it doesn't make sense, then. 'Cause it didn't get up and walk out of here by itself," Nowak argued.

I glared at her in a way that said to back down. What didn't she understand about keeping quiet and letting me ask the ques-tions? "Nowak, we get it. You want an answer regarding the whole tragedy, but I trust that if anyone saw the injector, they'd be glad to let you know. One thing that's bugging me, though, is how did Ray get exposed to peanuts in the first place." I tried to sound casual.

"Yeah, I'd like to know, too." Dickey put his cards facedown. "Was it your lady friend's food?"

"Trust me, Bezu was super careful in her food prep. She knew about his allergies, about everyone's dietary needs." I paused. "Did anyone see him before the tournament? Maybe he was somewhere beforehand and came in contact with the aller-gen. It could've been on his clothes or hands."

"You know, I did see him an hour or so before the tourna-ment, walking into the Bohemian Hotel," JJ remarked.

"Was he with anyone?" I asked.

"I didn't see anyone else." JJ took a chug of his beer.

"That couldn't have been Ray. He was at city hall before the game," Patrice said.

"Hmm. Maybe it was his doppelganger," JJ mused.

Tomorrow morning, I'd visit the Bohemian Hotel and city hall. I took a moment to think of how to frame my next question to the group.

"Does anyone here have any reason they wanted my uncle dead?" Nowak blurted out as a tear streaked down her face.

I hung my head and let out a breath, knowing the game was going to blow up, and I had no way to defuse it. My entire body felt like it melted into the chair.

"Hey! Wait a minute." Dickey eyed me and then Nowak. "Is that the real reason we're all here? Do you consider us suspects? Are you kidding me? No one likes being questioned under false pretenses."

"Is that what you're doing?" Patrice scowled at me as she threw her cards down on the table. "If you want to question me, make it official."

"Yeah. And it would be McFalls' case anyway." Howie got up from his chair. "José, seriously? We're all friends here."

Dickey stood. "I, for one, think you're treading on shaky ground here, José."

"I'm out of here." Patrice grabbed her purse. "Split the pot. Do whatever. As far as I'm concerned, this tournament is over, *for good*."

"I'm with you." JJ pointed his finger at me. "You really are a jerk."

Because Nowak had been eager and impatient, our questioning had headed south so quickly it made my head spin. There'd be no recovering from this.

"Sounds like tonight's a bust," Norman chimed in. He looked at the dealer. "Maggie, I'll square away with you for what I owe you before you leave."

"Hold on, everyone." Nowak stood. "José and I are not dropping this investigation until we know what happened to my uncle."

"Well, tough shit. You'll have to do it without us," JJ yelled as he marched away.

CHAPTER 17

"I'd say they were all a bit too sensitive last night, don't you think, Sergeant?" Nowak asked as we walked into the lobby of the Bohemian Hotel the next morning.

"You accused them of murder. What did you think was going to happen? They would be happy? That one of them would raise their hand and say 'I did it'?" I chided her.

She blushed. "Perhaps I didn't approach them the right way."

"No kidding," I grumbled under my breath as we entered the elevator.

She leaned against the mirror-lined wall and sighed. "How else will I find out?"

"Certainly not by pissing people off. It's not the best way to conduct an investigation. And some of those people are my friends, I'd like them to still speak to me after this is over." I pushed the button for the bar and restaurant.

"Sorry." She looked down at her feet like a child who had just been scolded.

When my dog had been a pup and chewed up my favorite shoes, he'd had those big eyes and eager-to-please attitude that made it hard for me to stay angry. I felt the same way about Nowak, even though she was a pain in my ass.

"Chin up, Nowak. Just let me do the talking from now on.

Watch and learn. Consider yourself a silent partner. Emphasis on *silent*."

She started to speak but then stopped and nodded.

"Well, that's a good start." I smiled at her as we exited the elevator.

The sound of tinkling glasses greeted us as we made our way into the restaurant. Floor-to-ceiling glass windows on three sides afforded panoramic views of the Savannah River. The kitchen was in a far corner, a metal swinging door separating it from the dining room. A bar sat in the middle of the room, and there were silver chairs with wooden tables arranged both inside and on an outside deck. Near the bar, three workers dressed in black pants and white tops were wrapping utensils in white napkins.

"Good morning." I introduced Nowak and myself and flashed my badge. I was uneasy about it because, technically, I shouldn't be doing this. "I know you're all busy. And this is a long shot, but I'd like to know if you all remember someone who was in here early Friday afternoon."

The three of them looked at Nowak and me. A brunette with large green eyes put down a tray of silverware. "I'm Amanda. I worked that shift. But I can't promise you I'll remember anything. We get a lot of people here."

"I know it's a slim chance, but I'm trying to fill in a timeline on someone. It's important to know what he did on Friday," I explained. "Any information at all would be appreciated."

"Okay." Amanda nodded. "I have a minute."

After finding a picture of Ray on my phone from a ceremony we both attended several months ago, I showed it to her. "See that guy?" I pointed to Ray. "Did you happen to see him here?"

Nowak leaned over my shoulder.

Amanda squinted. "Yeah, I remember him. Only 'cause he made quite a scene."

"What happened?" I asked.

"We need every single detail," Nowak added.

I rolled my eyes at Nowak, who mimed locking her lips and throwing away the key.

"I remember he had some sort of fight with the lady he was with," Amanda told us. "He seemed kind of like a bully."

"He's *dead*. And he was my *uncle*." Veins in Nowak's neck stood out. She clenched her fists.

Unfortunately, she seemed to have found the key to her mouth.

I turned to Nowak, putting my hand out. "I got this." I'd noticed this a few times, Nowak's trigger point when someone talked bad about Ray.

"I'm so sorry," Amanda stammered.

"Listen, you didn't know." I had to get Amanda to continue this conversation and not hold back because she was afraid of offending Nowak. "What did the woman look like? Anything that stood out to you?"

"She had big dark sunglasses on and a scarf over her hair. It was obvious she was uncomfortable being seen with him," Amanda recalled.

"Was she tall or short? Thin or heavy?" I encouraged her to remember more.

"She was sitting down. Average weight. Average everything, I guess." Amanda paused. "But you know, there was one thing that stood out. Her nails were painted red, white, and blue."

Nowak nodded.

"Did you overhear their conversation?" I asked.

"Bits and pieces. He seemed pissed. I heard her say something about moving. Maybe that's what set him off. I'm not sure." Amanda tugged at the sleeve of her shirt. "He raised his voice and grabbed her arm. Then I said, 'cause I don't put up with that bully crap, I said, 'I'm calling the cops.' Then he was, like, 'I am a cop. Leave it alone.' After that, he chilled a bit, and the lady left."

"What happened after she left?" I asked.

"He sat there for a minute. Drinking his beer." Amanda returned to her task, picking up a fork, knife, and spoon followed by a linen napkin. She rolled the silverware inside and then placed it on a pile of completed napkins. She glanced at her phone. "Listen, I'm sorry, but I really have to finish setting up."

"If you don't mind, just one more question. Did he have anything to eat?"

"I don't think so. He might have had some of the pretzel mix we put on the bar." Amanda pointed toward the bar. "I'm not sure. I didn't keep an eye on him the whole time."

"Does the mix have any peanuts in it?"

"Not sure."

Nowak seemed to take the cue and walked over to the bar.

I thanked Amanda before Nowak and I left.

On the way back down the elevator, Nowak told me, "There were pretzels, sesame sticks, goldfish cheese crackers, and rye chips in the mix. No peanuts."

"And he didn't order any other food, so right now I doubt he had contact with the allergen here. Besides, it's a long shot that he would have a reaction so long after getting exposed."

"You're right." Nowak exited the elevator with me, and we made our way to the hotel lobby. "I know what we need to do next."

I thought I'd let her tell me.

Nowak wiggled her fingers. "It's the nails."

"Go on," I prompted.

"It's the only clue, really."

"Yeah. I know. Not much to go on."

"There are a lot of nail salons around. And a lot of women getting manicures, so there's no way to track the mystery woman down through her salon."

"You're right. What would you do next?" I wanted her to use logic and deduce the following step.

"We need to visit Councilwoman DeLeon. She knew Ray. Last night, I noticed she had the same nail polish that Amanda described. She very well might be the mystery woman." The door whooshed open and we made our way outside. "As the police academy taught us, go with the obvious first, before the obscure."

When she wasn't emotional, she was clever. I smiled. "You're pretty smart, rookie."

She beamed as if I had given her a gold medal.

CHAPTER 18

"*W*hat a surprise seeing both of you," Patrice greeted us. After closing her office door behind us, she motioned for us to sit and then half-laughed. "Do I need to get a lawyer before I speak to you?"

"No, of course not." I folded myself into a narrow, padded chair opposite her desk, meanwhile noting Patrice's patriotic nails.

Nowak sank into the chair next to mine.

"After the way the game ended last night, with your ambush interrogation, I thought I needed to lawyer up before I spoke to you again." She glared at me. "You do realize you insulted me and probably everyone else there."

"We didn't mean to." I shot Nowak a glance.

"I'm really sorry. I didn't mean to, either. I've been very emotional with all that happened," Nowak explained.

"I understand you're going through a really tough time. I'm sorry for that. No need for apologies. We all say things we don't mean when we're upset. I've forgiven the unwarranted allegations." Patrice folded her hands on her desk and leaned forward.

Great, I thought, *just in time for me to accuse you of being Ray's mistress*. I'd have to handle this gently and get around to her relationship with Ray without offending her.

"So, what can I do for you?" Patrice asked.

Nowak leaned forward. "I want to know what you and my uncle were doing at the hotel."

So much for decorum and tact.

Patrice did everything but look at Nowak. It was obvious the question hit a nerve.

"What Nowak meant to say is that someone who looked like you met Ray at the Bohemian Hotel a few hours before Friday night's poker tournament. We were just wondering where you were before the game." I tried to sound nonjudgmental as I shot Nowak the evil eye.

Nowak blushed and fidgeted in her chair.

Apparently, she got my message.

"This is the second time you've insulted me. I don't need to answer you." Patrice stood.

I got up from my chair, too.

"It could've been anyone." She walked towards the door. "Ray was quite the charmer. I bet he had a lot of lady friends." She opened the door. "This meeting, or whatever it is, is over. I've got a lot to do."

Nowak followed at my heels.

Patrice folded her arms. "José, we've been friends for a long time. And you're good at your job. I know that. But what I don't get is why you're trying to turn an accidental death into some sort of investigation."

"There are a lot of loose ends. It's my job to find answers and tie them up," I argued.

"And it's personal to me," Nowak added.

"I know, and again, I am so very sorry about what happened to your uncle. I can't imagine what you're going through. You have my deepest sympathy." Patrice brushed at her hair. "By the way, you'll be hearing about this sooner or later, so I might as well tell you now. I'm leaving office at the end of the month and moving to Atlanta."

Surprised, I asked, "Are you staying in government?"

"No. I'm done with that." Patrice sighed. "I received a job offer in the private sector I couldn't refuse."

"Congratulations." I remembered Amanda saying that Ray's temper had flared after the mystery lady had said she was moving.

"How angry was my uncle when you told him?" Nowak asked, not beating around the bush.

It was apparent that Nowak was stubborn, letting her emotions about her uncle overtake her thinking.

"What Nowak is saying is that, right now, all the facts point to you as the mystery woman who met Ray at the Bohemian."

Patrice's mouth hung open, her eyes wide.

"C'mon, we're friends. You can level with me," I urged.

"I…um…well…" She bit her lip. "It's complicated."

"Try me," I persisted.

"Ray and I had a *relationship*." Patrice's voice lowered almost to a whisper.

"No kidding." Nowak rolled her eyes.

I looked at Nowak and mouthed, "Shut up."

"I know the hypocrisy, committing adultery while my campaign slogan was 'always doing what's right.'" Patrice hung her head. "You don't need to admonish me any more than I already have. I put my marriage, career, and—well, everything on the line. Ray was charming. I was foolish and weak. But—" Patrice looked away.

"You had an affair," I guessed.

"Yes." She stopped. "But you have to understand that I wanted out of it. I met him at the Bohemian before the tournament, and I told him I was resigning from office. I also told him I'd come clean to my husband. That there was nothing left to hold over me. But Ray didn't want to hear any of that." She shook her head. "He was so angry at me. He grabbed my arm and told me I could never get out. I *owed* him."

"Owed him?" I leaned against the door.

"After our relationship started, he began to blackmail me. He said that he would expose me if I didn't do *favors* for him."

"You were his pawn in City Hall, weren't you? You pushed his promotion through over mine, didn't you?" I felt anger boil in my blood. It should have been my decision if I accepted or rejected the promotion. It had been mine to make, not hers.

"I'm so sorry, José." Patrice looked at me, her eyes brimming with tears. "I felt like I had no choice; I was so tangled up in the deception. It was the biggest mistake of my life."

"Is that how I got on the bomb squad?" Nowak asked.

Patrice slowly nodded.

"There were other cops more qualified than me. All this time, I wondered why I got the assignment." Nowak's shoulders slumped. "I was hoping it was because I deserved it."

"It doesn't matter now." I felt sorry for the kid. "I'll make you great. By the end of training, you'll have earned your spot on the team just like anyone else."

Nowak half smiled at me.

I turned back to Patrice. "And I'm paying for your favors, too, because I didn't make lieutenant and get the raise that went with it." My voice rose as I continued. "How many times have you screwed people? Messed up their career, like mine?" My jaw compressed.

"I'm so sorry." A tear trickled down Patrice's' cheek, and she wiped it away.

"Well, that won't change what you did to me." I glared at her while my neck muscles tensed up. "You, of all people. You were supposed to be my friend."

"You were my friend. I messed up. I get that you're pissed, and you have every right to be."

"That's the understatement of the day." I looked away from her.

"José, if I could go back and change everything, trust me, I would," Patrice said in a low, soft tone. "My marriage is over, and there's no changing that."

"Karma sucks." As soon as I said it, I regretted it, knowing how snarky it sounded.

"I deserved that, José. I cost you your promotion. Not only that, I betrayed my marriage vows. I lowered my values and ethics on so many levels. That's why I told Ray that I had to leave

Savannah, start fresh. That I didn't care what he did to me. I was done doing his bidding."

"The night he died, you grabbed his phone to wipe away any trace of your relationship," I realized. "Covering your ass."

"You're right." Lowering her gaze, Patrice put a hand on my arm. "But I had nothing at all to do with his death. Zero. You have to believe me. I might be an adulterer, but I'm not a murderer. Trust me."

"*Trust a politician.* Do you even hear yourself?" I twisted away from her touch. "Worried about appearances. Once a politician, always a politician."

"You're mad. I get that. You should be. You hate me now, and I don't blame you. I totally messed up. One day, I hope you'll find it in your heart to forgive me. But that's up to you. I can't change anything in the past." Patrice glanced toward Nowak. "I'm so sorry about what happened to your uncle. I really am."

"Me too." Nowak's eyes welled up as she turned away from Patrice.

"Now that it's over, and I'm leaving, I don't see the point in letting my *indiscretion* come out," Patrice reasoned. "I'd like to leave my reputation intact."

"You don't deserve that. You made your bed; you have to lie in it, whether it's here or in Atlanta." I grimaced. "But let me be perfectly clear, our friendship is over."

"I know," Patrice murmured.

I still needed to find out how Ray had gotten exposed to peanuts. "There's one more thing I need to know. Did Ray tell you where he was going once he left the Bohemian?"

"Why do you want to know?" Patrice frowned.

"Hey, you just admitted you cost him his promotion. The least you can do is answer his question." Nowak puffed her chest out. "He's trying to figure out how my uncle got exposed to peanuts, that's all."

"Forgive me. You're right." Patrice sighed. "And no, he didn't tell me."

CHAPTER 19

"*W*ell, that meeting was weird and not at all useful in figuring out what happened to my uncle." Nowak and I walked along River Street. "Let's grab some lunch now. I'm starved."

I glanced at the few dozen stands set up along the river. Some had white canopied tops protecting them from the glaring sun. Their occupants peddled food and local souvenirs while a band played country music. Throngs of people milled about the area. River Street seemed to have some sort of festival going on almost every weekend. A group of guys walked by. I turned my head and checked out the tall, dark-haired one before quickly looking back.

"Hey, what was that about?" Nowak asked.

"What?"

"Were you checking that guy out?" Nowak shrugged. "I mean, I've noticed you do that before. I don't give a damn and all, and it's really none of my business, but I'm just connecting dots, being observant like we're trained to be in the academy. If you're gay, it's no biggie. Really."

I averted my eyes.

Maybe Bezu, Annie Mae, and Cat were right. Maybe I should

simply be honest about who I was. It was apparent I couldn't control my reaction when I saw a handsome guy. I thought I'd been doing such a great job of concealing my attraction to men. Maybe I'd have to work harder to hide my inclination.

"There wouldn't be anything wrong with it, you know. Not in this day and age. I'm just saying. It's none of my business, but if you are, you don't have to hide it from me." Nowak hesitated. "But I can tell you don't want to talk about it, so I'll stop now."

She was right that being gay in general society wasn't as big of a deal now as it once had been. But things were different in the police world. There were a bunch of Neanderthal cops on the force. I changed the subject. "We're no closer to finding out how Ray came in contact with the allergen."

"No kidding."

"Maybe after we eat, we could check Ray's car. See if there's anything in there that might have been contaminated. It's a long shot, but it's all we've got."

"I've got his spare set of car keys," Nowak offered.

"Good."

She inhaled loudly. "Can lunch wait a minute?"

"Yeah. Why?"

"Don't you smell that? Dessert first." Nowak pulled out her wallet. "Sweet baked wonderfulness. Funnel cakes. My treat."

A loud crack pierced the quiet from somewhere to my left. The noise of the bullet whizzed past my ear.

"Get down!" I screamed as I tackled Nowak to the ground. I unholstered my gun, scanning the area as I placed myself between her and the shooter. "Are you okay?"

"Twisted a bit." Nowak held her ankle. "But, yeah. I'm good."

"Everyone! Take cover!" I yelled as loudly as I could. There were hundreds of people in the line of fire, and no way to tell who the target was. Grabbing Nowak's wrist, I dragged her toward a short brick wall enclosing a large flowerbed.

Two more shots rang out as we ran, bits of cement dust and debris exploding from the sidewalk in front of us where the bullets impacted. They seemed to follow us. Shoving Nowak down behind the wall, I crouched low and searched for the shooter. With the crowd in a frenzy to get to safety, it didn't take long for me to pinpoint the likely suspect.

Someone in a dark hoodie was moving too slowly to be in the same fear for his life as an innocent bystander. He shoved what looked like a pistol into his pocket.

"I've got eyes on the shooter. You okay?" I whispered, never taking my eyes off the suspect in the hoodie.

"Go. I'll call backup and secure the area," Nowak assured me.

I ran in the direction of the shooter, who kept his head down and face out of sight. My approach obviously caught his attention, though, as he immediately took off in a sprint.

I gave chase but almost tripped over a group of girl scouts spilling out of a souvenir shop.

"That was so cool! I didn't know they were filming a movie today," a girl exclaimed, beaming.

An adult in the group remarked, "I hope they do that again, so we can take pictures."

I weaved around the group, yelling at them, "This isn't a movie. Take cover now!"

As I ran along the cobblestone streets, dodging cars and pedestrians, I kept a visual on the shooter, who was about a hundred feet ahead of me. As usual, River Street was packed, but most of the tourists and locals had already scattered.

The muscles in my legs burned from exertion, but I ignored the pain. I was catching up with the guy and would have him within reach soon. As though hearing my thoughts, the shooter accelerated and then ducked into an alley.

I followed him and rounded the corner of Factors Walk, the back side of the buildings that face River Street. He dodged a car and then scrambled away. As I followed him, the smell from the alley dumpsters rotting in the heat made me gag and my eyes water.

The shooter raced up the steep brick steps leading to Bay Street.

Adrenaline pumped through me as I raced up the stairs, two

at a time. He had on faded, ripped baggy jeans, blue-and-yellow gym shoes, and a dark gray hoodie that covered his head. Between five ten and six feet and on the average side regarding build. I caught a glimpse of his face and saw he wore what looked like a wrestling mask.

A cluster of prom kids—girls in long gowns and guys in tuxes—gathered on the iron walkway connecting the buildings, snapping selfies. For a moment I thought I'd lost my suspect until one of the girls screamed. "Hey, you creep!"

The shooter bolted out from behind the cluster of teens.

I chased after him until he made it across the street and then zoomed into a shop. Entering the store, I felt cool air blast my face as I scanned the area. The narrow aisles were crammed with displays of postcards, T-shirts, souvenirs, and other tourist treasures. Shoppers populated the little remaining open space.

Damn it, where was he? Dread filled my chest that I'd lost him. Then an alarm sounded, indicating a back door had opened. He must have exited.

Darting to the back of the store, I flashed my badge at the employee who was in the process of shutting off the alarm. Exiting, I whipped my head from left to right. A cluster of people gathered outside of a bar. Passing in front of them was a family pushing strollers. No hoodie guy running anywhere. He was gone. The back alley was empty.

How did I lose him? I turned back and saw a garbage can with its lid cockeyed. A piece of fabric protruded. Taking a pen from my pocket, I hooked the lid and lifted it off to set it on the ground. Then I used the pen to poke around the contents heaped on top. There was the dark gray hoodie. Wrapped inside it was a mask and gun. He'd gotten away, and I had no decent description of him. He could've been standing right next to me, and I wouldn't know him.

"The shooter seemed to be after either Nowak or me." I was standing next to McFalls in the alley.

"Are you sure of that? That this guy was gunning for you specifically?" McFalls asked.

"The first shot could have been random. But when we moved, shots followed us," I explained.

"Who was behind you?"

"I don't remember. I was too busy looking for the shooter. When I spotted him, I took off."

"If you don't know who was in your immediate area, the gunman coulda been after someone else. A gangbanger maybe. A drug dealer. We have no way of knowing right now. I'll look into it." He shook his head. "Shit. Let's hope we don't have a wannabe cop killer on the loose."

"No kidding," I agreed.

"Thankfully, no one was hurt." McFalls bagged the gun. He had already bagged the hoodie and mask. "I'll see if the gun was registered. The officers on River Street have already secured the area and recovered a couple of slugs. We'll send them to ballistics and cross-check for matches."

I had given him all the physical details of the shooter that I recalled. "Can you check social media, see if anyone posted pictures around the time it happened? Maybe some tourist got a photo."

"Yup. I already have a team working on it." McFalls zipped the bag with his gloved hand. "More than likely, though, it was gang-related. Our unit has been working nonstop to find members, get them off the street and locked up. One gang wears masks like this." He held up the bag with the mask in it. "So that's my hunch. Hell, last night WSAV broadcast an investigative report on Savannah gangs. Anybody could've seen the same report. For all I know, we could have a damn copycat on our hands."

There were too many coincidences. Nowak and I had questioned the staff at the Bohemian about Ray and then visited Patrice at her office to uncover details of Ray's final day. It was shortly after leaving her office that the shots had been fired at us. I thought we were stirring up something that someone wanted to keep concealed. "My gut says that what happened could be related to Ray's death."

McFalls exhaled. "C'mon, José, you're a great cop. Get off that whole theory. Do I have to spell it out to you? Ray's death was an A-C-C-I-D-E-N-T. Besides, you're bomb squad, not homicide. Stay out of it. Remember, I told you I'm taking care of it."

Next time, I'd keep my thoughts to myself.

ON MY WAY TO RAY'S MEMORIAL SERVICE, MY CELL RANG.

"José, you busy?" Regina asked.

"I've always got time for you." I pulled over and parked on the side of the road under a shady oak tree.

"Did you locate Ray's EpiPen?"

"No. Did you find out anything more from his autopsy?"

"Actually I did," Regina told me. "There was peanut residue around his injection site."

"That explains the anomaly you told me about before. But how do you think the allergen got there?" This made me even more convinced that Ray's death was not an accident.

"No. That's why I need the EpiPen."

"Why would there be peanut oil on the shot?"

"I've been wondering, too. It could've been on his hands, his pant leg—there are lots of possibilities. There was also residue on his coat jacket pocket where he kept the shot. I think a lot of questions can be answered, and theories ruled out, once we have the device."

"It really is the Holy Grail now." I repeated what Norman had said before. "Dickey did research and found that there were faulty injectors, so he wants it as well. Trust me, I'm doing my best to find it. But peanut oil around the injection site is a big development."

"Yes. But we need to trace where the peanut residue could have come from."

"Don't I know it." I thought about the last few hours of Ray's life, at the Bohemian Hotel bar with Patrice, then at the poker game. What I knew was that he'd come into contact with the allergen somewhere along the way. I needed to narrow down the time. "Do you know how long it takes to have an allergic reaction after contact with the allergen?"

"Symptoms can start a few minutes after exposure. But they can show up as long as two hours after. Sometimes the symptoms go away, and a second wave hits—a biphasic reaction. Although, given what I've learned through the autopsy, I doubt that Ray experienced the second wave."

"So, based on what you just said, Ray must've been exposed two hours or less before he died."

"Yes. I'd say that's correct."

Thinking of Bezu's concern, I had to ask Regina. "So, the allergen could have been in his food?"

"I've ruled that out. There was no indication in his saliva or his stomach that he had ingested peanuts."

"That's good news for Bezu. She was worried she might have accidentally used peanut oil in the muffins." I'd call Bezu with the news as soon as I finished the conversation.

"Based on my medical expertise, Bezu can rest easy." Regina stopped. "But that still leaves wide open the question of how he came in contact with the allergen that night."

"You're telling me. This has been on my mind nonstop since he died." I inhaled a deep breath and then let it out. "I think it must've happened right before or during the poker tournament. The span of time from us beginning the game to when he went into anaphylactic shock was just under two hours."

"That's a reasonable time frame from exposure to symptoms."

"Which makes me think one of two things. One, Ray had the allergen on him right before he entered the tournament, or two, someone in that room exposed him to peanuts." I would bet that same person had shot at Nowak and me.

"Sounds like you've got your work cut out for you."

"Yes, ma'am." Based on McFalls' reaction, I knew Nowak and I had to go rogue for this investigation.

Out of the ten of us in the room that night, all of us had had the means and opportunity. A strong motive would separate the innocent from the guilty. Taking Ray, Bezu, and myself out left seven suspects.

CHAPTER 20

"*U*ncle Ray was in the first row of every one of my games or school functions. He didn't miss a single one." Nowak spoke from the podium at Ray's evening memorial service.

As was the case for anyone on the force who died, nearly the entire police department attended, along with the mayor, local elected officials, state and federal officials, and other government employees. In consequence, the pews were packed in the downtown church. For the past hour or so, Howie had sat by my side during the formal full-honors ceremony. We were now hearing the eulogy. Ray's sister had spoken after the police chief and was followed now by her daughter, Nowak.

"I could always count on my Uncle Ray, who was like a father to me. His heart was so kind and open," Nowak told the crowd. Like all of us, she wore her full uniform.

"Open zipper, more like, screwing my wife," Howie muttered to me under his breath.

"You were separated," I whispered back, hating that he was being disrespectful during the memorial. "It sucked that it happened, but get over it."

"Never will. Good riddance," Howie loudly whispered.

"Now is not the time," I chided in a hushed tone.

"Last month, my wife and I ran into him at the grocery store, and he started flirting with her. Right in front of me. The jerk pushed my buttons."

He was talking in an audible whisper now, and he didn't seem to want to stop. I had to get him out of here. Since we were in the last row, I motioned for Howie to follow me out into the vestibule.

"I just can't sit in there and act like I give a shit that he died." Howie shook his head. "I had to be here, or I'd look like a big jerk for not honoring one of our own."

"But you were out of line talking like that in there. It was disrespectful. Can you just shelve it for now?"

"No, I can't. You don't know how Ray got to me. What he did with my wife still makes me crazy. I can't help myself."

"You know he wasn't all bad. He was an incredible uncle to Nowak. He was a good cop. He had issues, I know. But he wasn't one hundred percent asshole."

"Hmph." Howie leaned against a wall. "Maybe ninety-nine percent."

Howie had a motive to kill Ray. I'd hate to think of him as a potential suspect in Ray's death, but he'd been one of the players at the poker tournament. And the fact that he was a friend didn't mean I could rule him out.

"We are here to celebrate his life, his many accomplishments here in Savannah. Just as the mayor mentioned during his speech earlier, Ray made this city safer by getting criminals off the street and behind bars." Nowak's voice came over the speaker into the church vestibule, where Howie and I stood. The scent of lit candles mixed with the smell of polish on the heart pinewood floors.

"Yeah. One of his convicts just rode the needle," Howie said under his breath.

I was thankful we were now out of earshot, and no one could hear his remarks.

Howie was referring to the criminal Ray had put away for murder fifteen years ago and who'd been put to death the other day by lethal injection. "It was a big case, and he did a great job on that," I told Howie. "You heard the mayor; that case made Ray's career. Ray's work was solid—it stood up even after multiple appeals."

"Really? That's how you feel about him? He's some sort of a hero?" Howie shook his head. "He was nothing but a jerk. I heard his dad didn't even show up today."

I thought of how it would tear me apart if I didn't have a relationship with my father. His opinion of me meant the world. I wouldn't do anything that could jeopardize it. Like come out. "That's sad that his father chose not to attend."

"Yeah."

"Ray shouldn't have died." I kept a close eye on Howie's physical reactions.

Howie waved his arms around. "But he did, and here we all are."

"Yeah." I paused. "It was such a weird accident—it was almost too *coincidental*."

"Seriously?" Howie stepped back and held his hands up. "Are you doing this again? Your witch hunt?"

"No, no," I lied. "There are some things that simply aren't making sense, and I want to make sure I get answers to my questions."

"By the way, if you're even considering for one nanosecond that I had anything to do with his death, then you're barking up the wrong tree. Yeah, I hated the guy, but damn it, I'd never kill anyone. C'mon, José, you've known me forever. How could you even think I'm capable of that? It was a tragic accident, nothing more."

"Yeah, I know. But what if it wasn't? I think the shooter on River Street was after Nowak or me."

"I heard about the shots on River Street and that you and the rookie were there. That can spook even the best of us. This city has gone to shit with all the gangs. Thank goodness no one was hurt."

"No kidding. We recovered clothing and the gun the shooter dumped. Maybe we'll get a lead on that soon."

"I hope so." Howie paused and then added, "You know, even

on the outside chance there's more to Ray's death than an accident, you'd have nothing to do with it anyway. It would be McFalls' case."

He had no idea that my involvement had become personal. "Yeah, I know."

"Do me a favor and let it lie. Ray's going in the ground today. I suggest you bury whatever questions you have about his death, too."

I nodded, although I had no intention of burying anything.

CHAPTER 21

*A*fter updating Nowak on the investigation, I told her that I'd interview those who'd attended the poker tournament. She was busy with family in town for the memorial service, and I didn't want her to worry about the inquiry.

After leaving the memorial, I headed to the Magnolia Club to visit Norman and Big Mike, the next two on my list to question. My gut said that they weren't suspects. Yet I had to talk to them and make sure they could be ruled out.

The line outside the Magnolia Club was long, and a few people remarked about my cutting ahead. I flashed my badge, although I felt a bit guilty doing it since I wasn't there on truly official business.

"Hey, what's up?" Big Mike asked while he carded a guest at the door by shining a light at the ID.

"Sweetie Pie always draws a crowd, doesn't she?"

"Yup." He carded another guest.

"Do you have a minute? I'd really like to talk to you," I said.

"Sure. Let me get someone to take over here." He set his flashlight down on the barstool and waved another bouncer to the door.

We moved inside beyond the club's front door.

Big Mike grabbed a bottle of water and then turned to me. "What do you need?"

"You remember Nowak, Ray's niece?"

"Yeah."

"She's having a real hard time with her uncle's death."

"I bet she is, poor kid."

"Truth be told, I'm troubled over how Ray died and wondering if you could help me clear a few things up."

"Not sure how much I can help, but I'll try." He inclined against a wall.

"The night Ray died, did you see any peanuts or peanut oil anywhere?"

"Nope. There aren't any in the bar that I know of." Big Mike took a swig from his water bottle.

"I believe that Ray came in contact with his allergen sometime during the game." I ran a hand through my hair.

Big Mike straightened his back. "Oh?"

"It could've been an accident, a chain of one bad event after another."

Big Mike shook his head. "Shitty luck."

What I needed to find out was Big Mike's history with Ray. See if Big Mike had a grudge against him. "Seemed like you knew Ray already."

"Sort of. I'd seen him around here and there during the past couple of years or so. I didn't know him really well, though."

For a second, I wondered why Ray had spent a lot of time in the club. Could he have been gay? He certainly seemed homophobic. Maybe he overcompensated with a macho demeanor to cover who he really was. I focused back on Mike. "Didn't Ray cause you to lose your job?"

"Yeah, that was last year. I was a bouncer at a dive bar down the street. But then I got this job after, and it's much better. It all worked out. He tried to get me canned from this one, too, but that didn't happen. Just to get Ray off his back, my boss told him that he'd fire me. I had to play along, but as you can see, I still have my job."

"Yes, I see that."

"You know, I think Ray was a garden-variety homophobe. Since I work here, and Norman performs here, he had it in for us. He thought this place was filled with nothing but flaming homosexuals. But that's not our only clientele. We get lots of straight tourists and locals in here, too. Like you, for example."

Inside, I cringed. Here I was, lying again. Hiding. Maybe one day, who I was wouldn't matter. I could be myself and not care what anyone thought. And maybe no one would care. But not now. "Ray could be a really big pain in the ass, though. He pissed off a lot of people."

"He did that to me *all the time.*"

"Sometimes when a person gets really mad, they can break. Snap. Do something crazy they normally wouldn't do."

"Like what? Kill someone who pisses them off?" He laughed. "Yeah, no doubt he aggravated me. But really, José, I don't make a habit of going around and hurting everyone who was ever a dick to me. Not in my job description."

A few feet away from us, a ruckus began at the main door.

"Looks like I'm needed," Big Mike noticed. "You staying for the show? Sweetie Pie is the MC tonight."

"I plan on it." I glanced around. Tables were filling up. Music played, and the strobe lights flickered patterns on the walls. "So, where is he?"

"Right behind you." Big Mike grinned before he left.

"They let anyone in here, don't they?" Sweetie Pie said when I turned around.

"Speak of the devil." I smiled.

"Only if he wears heels and a boa." Sweetie Pie gave me a hug. "I've got a few minutes before the show. Let me buy you a drink."

We walked over to the bar and gave our order to the same bartender from the other night, Elias.

For a few minutes, Sweetie Pie and I caught up.

Eventually, I steered the conversation to the real reason for my visit. "You know, today was Ray's memorial."

"I heard." Sweetie Pie sighed. "Not that I cried over it. I mean, we weren't friends, but all the same, it's awful that he died."

Elias placed our drinks in front of us.

"You know, speaking about Ray, I'm trying to get straight in my own mind what happened." I pulled my beer mug closer to me.

"You mean his death? Anaphylactic shock. You know that." Sweetie Pie shook his head.

I raised an eyebrow as I looked at him.

"I know that look, José. What's going on?" Sweetie Pie asked.

"Just some loose ends that are bothering me, that's all."

"Like what?"

"How Ray got exposed in the first place. And why the EpiPen didn't work."

"Could the allergen have been in his food?"

"Nope. It wasn't that. It had to be something else he came in contact with during the tournament."

"Just so you know, I haven't had peanuts in my bar for months now. Too much liability," Sweetie Pie asserted. "Sanders' Tavern is peanut-free."

I cleared my throat. "Which makes this all the more complicated. There was peanut residue on his clothing and around the injection site."

"You're thinking it was more than just an accident, aren't you?"

Nodding, I touched my nose. "It smells like murder."

"Seriously?" Sweetie Pie looked incredulous.

"Yeah, that's my theory. His hands had peanut oil residue. Maybe it was on the chips, cards, or his clothing."

"It was *my* poker set. Trust me, it was clean. Plus, we opened a brand-new deck of cards for the game. He must've gotten something on his hands somewhere else."

"Yeah. Maybe. That's what I'm trying to figure out. If I could find the EpiPen, that would help a whole lot."

"Still missing?"

"Yup. Seems to have disappeared into thin air."

Sweetie Pie finished his beer. "If your theory is true, why isn't Homicide on this?"

"Because Ray's death is not being investigated that way." I

took a drink of my beer and shrugged. "That's why Nowak and I took it upon ourselves to tie up the loose ends. Obviously, it's very personal to her."

Sweetie Pie flipped his boa over his neck. "What do you plan to do?"

"Talk to everyone who was at the tournament. Well, those who will still talk to me. I seem to have pissed off a bunch of people the last time we all got together." I leaned back on the barstool. "Speaking of that, I know how to get a hold of everyone but the dealer."

"I can help you with that. The dealer is the bartender's sister." Sweetie Pie called over the counter, "Hey, Elias, what's your sister's phone number? I had it written down but don't have it handy."

Elias stopped wiping the bar counter near us and glanced over at Sweetie Pie. "She just changed carriers and has a new one. I don't know it offhand. Can I get it to you later?"

"Sure." Sweetie Pie waved a hand. "And can you bring one more beer for my friend here? Put it on my tab."

Elias nodded and then turned toward the tap.

"I'm going to freshen up before the show," Sweetie Pie told me. "Why don't you relax and enjoy the night? You can get back to your Sherlock Holmes sleuthing after you watch marvelous me perform."

"Sure." I'd be watching, but my mind would be chasing my murder theory. After chatting with them, I couldn't imagine that either Norman or Big Mike had any motivation to kill Ray except the universal one: Ray was a jerk.

But if that had been the true motive, then someone would have killed him long ago. Mentally, I moved them further down my suspect list. Patrice had a motive, the blackmail, but I didn't think she had the wherewithal to do it as she easily caved to pressure. Killing someone would involve a load of pressure. That left four more people to talk to.

≈

Two hours later, after the show finished and the crowd dispersed to the back bar or to the upstairs dance area, a loud voice boomed from behind me.

"Where is Norman Sanders?" McFalls bellowed this as he flashed his badge at Big Mike. Following McFalls was Officer Taylor, a new cop on the homicide squad.

I approached them. "Hey, what's going on?"

"José, what are you doing here?" McFalls stopped. "You don't seem the type to hang out in a place like this."

I stiffened as though I were being attacked. "And what *type* is that?" I hoped he didn't notice my defensive tone.

"Easy there. I didn't mean anything by it. You and I both know this is a gay bar."

"That doesn't mean everyone in here is gay, McFalls. Lots of people enjoy the show."

"I got it. And for the record, I have nothing against gays. Hell, my cousin is gay."

I felt myself relax a bit. "Well, for the record, I just watched a friend in the show. Why do you need to see Norman?"

"You know where he's at?"

"He goes by Sweetie Pie here. More than likely, he's back in the dressing room." I thumbed behind me.

"Mind showing me where that's at?" McFalls asked.

I nodded. "Follow me."

McFalls and Officer Taylor trailed me to the back hallway. "So, are you going to tell me what's going on? I assume it's not a social visit."

"You'll find out in a minute."

Upon our entering the dressing room, Sweetie Pie looked over as he wiped makeup from his face. "Well, hello. To what do I owe this pleasure?" His blond wig and boa sat next to him on the vanity.

"Norman Sanders?" McFalls asked.

"Yes, that's me under all of this." Sweetie Pie winked.

"Would you mind if we looked around here?" McFalls put on gloves.

"I just might mind." Sweetie Pie crossed his arms. "What's going on? Why are you all here?"

"We received an anonymous tip. We're simply following through."

"A tip on what?"

He held up a search warrant. "Sorry, that I can't discuss. But I'd appreciate your cooperation." McFalls glanced around the room.

"It feels like I don't have a choice. So, suit yourself." Sweetie Pie glared at McFalls.

McFalls motioned to Taylor. "You look under the counter and in that pile next to it. I'll cover this area."

Sweetie Pie locked eyes with me.

I shrugged and shook my head. "Hey, McFalls, why don't you tell me what you're looking for so I can help out?"

"Thanks, but we got it." McFalls shoved the feather boa aside.

Taylor rummaged through some hanging clothes and then bent down to search in some bags lying on the floor.

With gloved hands, McFalls picked up a closed makeup case sitting on the counter. "Can you open this, please?" He pushed it toward Sweetie Pie.

"Of course, but powder-blue eye shadow would not look good on you. We have different coloring," Sweetie Pie observed.

McFalls didn't laugh but stared at Norman impassively.

Taylor, having finished his own search, stood next to Sweetie Pie.

Reluctantly, Sweetie Pie unzipped the case. He started to sit back, but something got his attention. He leaned forward and peered inside the case as McFalls rummaged around in it.

"Be careful," Sweetie Pie said. "That stuff costs a mint."

"I'm not sure what you think is in there—" I began just as McFalls paused and pulled out an EpiPen.

Holding it up, he said, "Norman Sanders, you're under arrest for suspicion of murder."

Officer Taylor cuffed Norman.

"How did that thing get in my makeup bag? It's not mine!"

Norman shouted. "It wasn't in there earlier this evening when I was getting ready."

"You'll have plenty of time to tell us your side at the station." McFalls nodded toward Taylor.

Taylor put a hand on Sweetie Pie's shoulder and guided him out the door while reading Norman his rights.

"This is a huge mistake. I have no idea how it got in there. José, help me!" Sweetie Pie called back as he was escorted through the bar. "I didn't kill anyone. I didn't like the guy, but no one did," Sweetie Pie choked out.

McFalls held up the bag with the EpiPen. "Looks like *evidence* to me."

"Really? Think about it. Norman would put the murder weapon in his own makeup case? That doesn't make sense," I pointed out.

"Criminals are dumb," McFalls claimed.

"What's his motive?" I asked.

"We'll figure that out when we question him." McFalls cleared a path through onlookers as he exited the bar.

"I didn't do anything; I'm not a killer!" Norman said.

"Keep your mouth shut until you talk to an attorney," I cautioned Norman as I followed them. Who made the call, and why now? I knew that Norman was innocent. That meant Ray's killer must have set Norman up. And that meant the killer must've been close by in order to have staged the evidence in Norman's makeup bag.

The killer was in the bar, lurking around in plain sight.

"Why are you telling him that?" McFalls glared at me. "Whose side are you on?"

"He's my friend, McFalls. I've known Norman a long time, and there's no way he killed Ray. As far as I know, he doesn't have a motive."

"As far as you know." McFalls repeated my words. "We'll know for sure once we talk to him. You might've been right this whole time, José, about there being more to Ray's death. Until now, we had nothing to go on."

"Who called it in?" I wanted to know.

"Some anonymous call on Crime Stopper."

"That's convenient, isn't it? Who would know to call except the real killer? Norman isn't guilty."

As we made our way outside next to the squad car, McFalls stopped. "We're friends, so I'm not going to tell anyone that you told a suspect not to talk to us. You're too close to this. Your perspective is being clouded by your friendship with the perp. I know how to do my job, so I suggest you back off and let me do it."

"You know as well as I do that there are flaws in the legal system that let guilty people go free and innocent people get locked up."

"I don't make mistakes." He opened the squad door and guided Norman into the backseat of the police cruiser.

As instructed, Norman remained silent.

Norman looked at me again.

I nodded and gave him a thumbs-up. Hoping to convey that I had his back.

He weakly nodded before he disappeared into the back of the police cruiser.

"Oh, and we executed a search warrant on Sanders' Tavern too. We have the poker chips and cards logged in as evidence. They're being tested as we speak. Our tipster said we'd find traces of peanut oil," McFalls informed me as he climbed into the driver's seat.

Had Norman lied to me? Did he really have it in for Ray, enough to commit murder? On the other hand, if Norman didn't do it, then that meant the killer had set him up.

Who would do that?

CHAPTER 22

Two hours later, McFalls was still grilling Norman in the precinct's interrogation room. It appeared he wouldn't let up until he got a confession. Norman's attorney sat adjacent to him. He'd hired Earl Chu, the handsome attorney with pitch-black hair and high cheekbones.

I stood behind the observation window the entire time, watching and listening to the interrogation.

McFalls held up the evidence bag containing the EpiPen. "Let's go over this again. Instead of epinephrine medicine, this shot was full of a blend of peanut oil that had the same consistency and color as EpiPen fluid. And you knew Ray was allergic to peanuts, correct?"

"Yes, I knew that. I told you. Everyone at the tournament knew that. Why aren't they in here, too?" Norman rubbed his eyes. "Can I go now? I'm so done with all of this."

"My client has been more than cooperative. I think we can wrap this up now," Earl agreed.

"Yes, we should. *Now*," Norman insisted.

"If you could indulge me just a few more minutes, I promise after that we'll be done. Okay?" McFalls said.

"If it will get me out of here, then fine. Five more minutes, that's it. I have nothing to hide. I'll prove my innocence and then get out of here. But right now I need some coffee," Norman complained. "Five minutes, not a second more."

"Fine." Earl leaned back in his chair.

McFalls looked at Taylor, who leaned against the door, "Can you get him a cup of coffee, please?"

"And if you can, add a few shots of Baileys to it," Norman added hopefully but then shook his head. "Never mind. Two sugars and a splash of cream will do."

After Taylor left, McFalls leaned forward. "Hey, between you and me, Ray could be a real ass, right?"

"You don't have to answer that," Earl told Norman.

"I don't mind." Norman shrugged.

"But as your counsel, I strongly suggest that—"

Norman interrupted his attorney and glared at McFalls. "Yeah, Ray was rough around the edges. He could be a royal ass."

"Watch what you're saying, Norman." Earl shook his head.

"It's okay. I've got this." Norman turned to McFalls and went on. "Ray was like that to everyone, not just to me. If you're implying that I killed him because he was an ass, then you should be interviewing a whole hell of a lot of other people, too."

"Except *you* were there when he died. *You* owned the poker set that was tainted with oil. *You* hosted the tournament at *your* establishment. *You* knew he was allergic to peanuts. And *you* had the EpiPen, full of peanut oil, in *your* possession. And I'm guessing that at some point during the night of the tournament, you switched your tampered EpiPen with Ray's real one." McFalls pointed at Norman. "It all leads back to *you* and *you* alone."

Norman hung his head and sighed. "We've been through this so many times in so many variations during however many hours I've been here." He slumped in his chair. "I never touched that shot, and I don't know how that damned thing got in my makeup bag."

The EpiPen was the smoking gun. The fact it had been found in Norman's possession made him the number one suspect.

To prove Norman's innocence, I needed to find the real killer.

It would help if I looked at the evidence myself. I left the observation room and walked next door to the crime lab. My forensic scientist friend Cody, nicknamed Beaker, was working.

He stood half a foot shorter than me, slightly hunched over, and wore black-rimmed glasses. His white lab coat seemed two sizes too big on his bony frame. Many years ago, we'd worked in this lab together.

Beaker looked up from his microscope. "Nice to see you, stranger. To what do I owe this pleasure?"

"Just popping by to say hi."

"Are you tired of explosives? Are you coming back to the dark side and joining us?"

"As good as that sounds, nope, I'm not." I looked around the room. I saw a pile of papers stacked on a desk. The trash was filled with discarded fast-food wrappers and drink cups. I could see that Beaker's love of junk food had not diminished. "I was wondering if you had anything logged in from McFalls regarding—"

"Ray's case?"

I nodded.

"Yes. It's high-priority. That's why I'm still here, working into the wee hours of the night."

"So, what can you tell me?"

I observed the familiar equipment on the countertops—a fume hood, chromatograph, and spectrometer. The room was brightly lit with overhead fluorescent lights, which shone a yellowish glow on the steel countertops. The walls were standard off-white, and the floor was a worn speckled linoleum. The place hadn't changed a bit since I'd worked here. And it still had the same hint of bleach scent.

"Why do you want to know?" he asked.

"I was there that night. Things aren't adding up," I said.

"What doesn't make sense? His EpiPen was filled with peanut oil."

"Yeah, I know."

"There's not one trace of fingerprints anywhere on it."

"Yeah. That bothers me. Why would Norman wipe it clean

and then place it in his own bag? If he really did it, why even keep the evidence at all? That doesn't make any sense."

"I guess not. But who knows what he was thinking? I still have to do more work on the case, but as you can see, I'm backlogged." He pointed to a countertop with dozens of boxes jampacked with plastic evidence bags. "The pile that looks like a mini Mount Everest."

I nodded. "Quite a backlog."

"You're telling me. I need, like, five of me working nonstop to get through all of them." He wiped his brow with the back of his hand. "I know your buddy got arrested for Ray's death."

"Yeah, he did. But he's innocent."

"Everyone that gets arrested says they're innocent."

"But Norman *really is*. And right now, it looks like I'm the only one who believes that. I'm trying to figure out what really happened that night."

"Good luck with that."

"Thanks for your vote of confidence." I watched as Beaker peered into the microscope.

"I mean, you're a great cop. If anyone can figure it out, you can. It's just that the odds are stacked against you, at least from what I can tell."

"Don't I know it. But I love a challenge." I also couldn't let an innocent man get put away for a crime he didn't commit. "I need to find out how Ray was exposed to the allergen in the first place. I think the key to finding the killer is discovering who planted the initial allergen exposure. Because I bet whoever did that also knew Ray would reach for his injector, and they had already replaced his real one with the altered one."

"Yeah, that's what happened. But finding out who did it—? Well, you've got your work cut out."

"I do. What about the peanut oil?"

"It was on the cards." Beaker took off his glasses and rubbed his eyes. Taking a corner of his lab coat, he cleaned his glasses with it and then put them back on.

"All of the cards?"

"Looks like it. Some more than others. I just tested them." He pointed to the table alongside him. "I have the report there."

"Would you mind if I take a look?"

Beaker raised an eyebrow. "I'm not too sure you should be doing that."

"Just a quick look. I promise."

"Fine, but if I get in trouble, I'm telling them you did this without my approval, okay?"

"Yup. Got it."

He walked over to his desk and grabbed a soda. "I heard you're going with Regina Fenny to my buddy's birthday cookout tomorrow."

"The eighties-themed one?"

He nodded and then drank from the can.

"Yeah, I got roped into going as repayment for a favor."

"I'm going as Indiana Jones. How about you?"

"Ponch, from *CHiPs*. Unless I can get out of it."

"Go, you'll have fun. Plus, I'll be there. We'll have time to catch up." Beaker's phone rang, and he took the call.

I took that as my cue and helped myself to the report.

The results showed that all the cards had oil on them, mostly concentrated on the edges. In the report, I read that three cards had more of their surfaces covered in the substance than the rest: a ten of clubs, a king of hearts, and a king of diamonds. I remembered Dickey mentioning that in the cards Ray had dropped, there'd been two kings.

The murderer was someone who'd had access to the cards, which we all had. But only the dealer would have been able to give Ray the ones saturated with the most oil.

Maggie must have had the oil on her hands, and it had been transferred onto the sides of the cards as she held the deck. When she'd dealt the cards to Ray, she'd swiped the fronts to make sure that he had full exposure to the allergen. Enough exposure to make him use his injector, with which she must have already tampered.

What I couldn't wrap my head around was why she would

kill him. I didn't know that yet. But I knew I was onto a solid lead.

Most crimes were committed because the victim and perpetrator had some connection. I needed to find out what linked Ray and Maggie.

It was time to have a talk with Maggie. Since I had no idea what her phone number was or where she lived, my first stop would be to talk to her brother Elias, the bartender at the Magnolia Club. I returned the report to where I'd found it.

I tapped Beaker on the shoulder. "Thanks."

He nodded as he continued his call.

A door opened, and Nowak walked in. "Someone told me they saw you come in here."

"I was just heading out. How you holding up?"

"Okay, I guess. Some relatives are still in town, but I'm over all the intense family time. Too much for me." She walked alongside me, keeping up with my brisk pace. "We're relieved McFalls found Ray's killer. I still don't know why Norman did it."

I let her talk.

"At least he'll be behind bars for what he did," Nowak continued. "Justice will be served, although it doesn't bring back my uncle."

How would I tell her Norman wasn't the killer and that I thought the real murderer could be Maggie? I stopped in my tracks.

She followed suit.

I let out a long exhale, knowing this would not be what she wanted to hear. But I had to tell her. "Here's the deal. I don't think Norman is guilty. Matter of fact, I'm almost positive."

Nowak locked gazes with me. "What do you mean? Yes, he's guilty. McFalls caught him red-handed with Ray's EpiPen. And Norman had run-ins with my uncle before."

"Yes, that's true. But I think the shot was planted on him."

"Why?"

I caught her up to speed.

"Maggie the dealer, why would she kill my uncle? That

doesn't make any sense to me. She didn't even know him. Didn't they only meet the night of the tournament?"

"Yes. At least I think so." I ran a hand through my hair. "But right now, all the clues lead to her, as far-fetched as it sounds. I'm going to pursue that lead until I find out otherwise."

"It just makes more sense that Norman did it. It was his bar, his cards, he didn't like my uncle…" She paused. "He had access to everything. He had a motive."

"I get it. And you can stay with that while I work on my theory." I continued down the hallway.

"Fine." She followed me. "But in case you're right, I'd like you to keep me in the loop. And please give me anything you might need help with, okay?"

"I can do that." I put my hand on the door leading to the parking lot.

"What's your plan?" Nowak asked.

"I'm heading to visit Maggie's brother at the Magnolia Club."

"Do you want me to go with?"

"Nope, I got it. I'll call you if I need anything."

"Thank you for all you're doing for my uncle. I know you didn't like him because he didn't treat you so well."

"It's not a matter of liking or not liking someone; it's a matter of finding the truth."

CHAPTER 23

"*H*ey, Big Mike." Upon entering the Magnolia Club, I greeted the bouncer. It was the morning after Norman's arrest. "Is Elias here?"

A pungent odor of an industrial lemon cleaner lingered in the air. Chairs were stacked on tabletops. A mop and bucket leaned against a wall.

"He's in the stockroom. He'll be out soon. How's Norman holding up?" Mike asked.

"Fine, considering." I glanced around the room. I heard some noise coming from the back and assumed that's where Elias was.

"You know, there's no way he killed Ray. I had more of a reason to do it than Norman had. Not that I did it, mind you." Big Mike took a chair from the tabletop, turned it over, and slid it by the table. "This whole thing with Norman sucks big-time."

I helped Big Mike pull the chairs from the tabletops and slide them under the tables. "I think he's innocent, too. But then that leaves the question of who did it."

"Yeah. Right now my buddy is being treated like a criminal. The way he was escorted out of here, everyone staring at him, that look on his face—" Big Mike stopped midsentence. "It's just not fair."

"I know. But after finding evidence in Norman's bag, they

had to take him in. I'm sure McFalls' team is doing a thorough investigation."

"Why aren't you all looking for the real killer, instead of picking on someone innocent?"

"Trust me. I'm doing the best I can to help him."

"You know what I think?" Mike rubbed his temples.

"Nope. I can't read minds."

Pulling a dolly stacked with cases of beer, Elias appeared in the doorway. He nodded as he passed.

"I gotta talk to this guy," I told Mike.

"But can you hold up a second?" Mike asked me.

"Sure." I watched Elias pull the dolly behind the bar and to the front of a huge refrigerator.

"Between you and me, I think someone put that shot thing in his bag," Big Mike declared.

"That's a theory I've already begun working on." I glanced around the room and saw only the one doorway from the main barroom into the back. "Did you see anyone go back there to the dressing room last night?" Someone who could have put the injector in Norman's case.

"It was busy. I really didn't pay attention."

"Do you have any video cameras here?"

"I wish. Like I told the other officers, they've been on the blink." He shook his head.

"Then there's no way to find out who might have snuck back there. Can you get me the names of everyone who was working?"

"Sure, I have a schedule back in the office." He put the last chair in place.

I patted Big Mike on the shoulder and left to approach Elias, who was in the process of loading bottled beers into the glass-front refrigerator. "Hi, Elias. Remember me?"

He looked up, one eyebrow raised. "Yeah. You're a cop."

"That's right. And I'm trying to get in touch with your sister, Maggie. Can I get her number and address?"

"Why are you asking so much about my sister?" He stopped

what he was doing and looked at me. "She hasn't done anything wrong."

"I'm just covering my bases. She was the dealer the night of the poker tournament, when the cop died."

He turned his back to me. "Give me a second." He finished unpacking the case he had been working on. Then he wrote down a number and address and handed the paper to me. "This should be her newest cell number, although I've tried calling her, and it didn't work. She's out of town now and might be in an area with crappy reception."

"Okay. Thanks. What's her last name?" I pulled up a barstool.

"Same as mine, Linzey."

I had him spell it out for me while I wrote it on the paper next to her number and address. I needed to find a connection between Maggie and Ray. "Do you know if she knew Lieutenant Ray Murphy before the night of the poker tournament?"

"Not that I know of." Elias shut the glass door. "She was hired just for that game." He stopped and folded his arms on his chest. "You know, I'm feeling uncomfortable talking to you about her."

"Yeah. I get it. No one wants to talk to a cop. But I'm not here in any official capacity. I'm just trying to help out a friend. Would you indulge me and let me ask a few more questions? Then I promise I'll get out of your hair."

"Fine." Elias shrugged his shoulders. "I guess."

"Did she have any other jobs?"

"Yeah, out of state in South Carolina. Some casino ship. Not sure if she still works there or not." Elias didn't make eye contact with me.

"Who does she hang out with?" Maybe a friend of hers had a beef with Ray, and Maggie had sought vengeance on his or her behalf.

"Not sure. I mean, besides me. But I work here all the time, so I don't get to see her a lot." He winced.

"You okay?"

"Chronic migraines. Some days are better than others. I'm so used to the pain, it's become normal to me. Only one med seems to help some."

125

"Sorry about that." I leaned my elbows on the bar. "Does your sister have a significant other?"

"Not that I know of." Elias grabbed a knife cutter and slit open a case of beer.

"How long has she lived here?" Maybe she'd had a run-in with Ray at some point. I needed to check her records.

"A few months." Elias had a gleam of perspiration on his forehead.

Was he getting nervous talking to me? Or was he hiding something, protecting his sister? "What brought her here?"

"She bounced around a lot, you know, going to where the jobs were. Guess there were jobs here."

"And her brother."

Elias looked away. "Yeah, that's right."

"Do you know where she lived before she moved back to Savannah?" I remembered that Norman had said she'd worked in Vegas, and I wanted to confirm that.

"Vegas." Elias turned his back to me. "I really have to get these stocked before we open tonight."

"Okay. Thanks for your help." I handed him my business card. "Please give my number to Maggie, and let her know I'd like to talk to her."

Big Mike walked over with a list of people who'd worked at the Magnolia Club the previous night, when Norman had been arrested. I thanked him before I exited the club. Outside, I took a picture of the list and sent it to Nowak. She'd wanted to be involved; I'd let her contact the employees.

A text came in from Regina. "See you tonight at six—*get into the groove!*" She also listed the address. I chuckled at the Madonna reference.

I tried to recall what I had on hand at my house to use for my Ponch from *CHiPs* costume. I had a pair of aviator sunglasses, tall black boots, and a motorcycle helmet. Thankfully, I had khaki pants and a matching short-sleeved button-down shirt as well. That would have to do. Admittedly, I hadn't put much thought into the event. But I did owe Regina, and I was a man of my word.

As I left, I punched in Maggie's number. *"The number you have reached is not accepting calls at this time."* The recorded message could mean any number of things, including an issue with service. Elias had said she was out of town. Maybe she was in an unserviceable area.

After talking to Elias, I felt I might be grasping at straws. If Maggie and Ray had only met that night, she would have had no cause to kill him. What would she gain by killing a stranger?

I wondered if Elias could be lying for her. Family members had been known to cover for each other, and I didn't know him that well.

What I did know for sure was that someone in the room that night had killed Ray. Based on what Regina had told me about allergen exposure and reaction time, I was confident Ray's exposure to the peanut oil had occurred after the dinner break because that's when he'd gone into anaphylactic shock. Where had everyone been around that time? I needed to account for everyone's whereabouts during the break, when I suspected the oil had gotten put on the cards.

On the evening of our tournament, the dinner break had lasted less than twenty minutes. Sanders' Tavern wasn't that big. There really wasn't any place to go that was out of sight except the restroom.

Coats hung on the back wall near the restrooms, in plain view. I doubted the killer would have had time to take the injector out of Ray's jacket, empty the medicine, refill it with peanut oil, and then replace it in the pocket without anyone noticing. What made more sense was that the killer had had another injector prefilled with peanut oil, which he'd swapped with Ray's epinephrine-filled injector. That sort of exchange could have taken place quickly and easily, without drawing attention. The killer then would have known that he or she only needed to expose Ray to enough allergen to get him to use his injector.

What details of that night was I missing?

Maggie had fanned the cards on the table before she'd left to eat. After that, anyone there could have come by the table and wiped oil on them. But how had Ray gotten the three cards with the most oil? Maybe the oil had instead been put on something he'd touched, like his glass or chair, then been transferred from his hands to his cards.

The question that kept coming back was, who had exposed Ray to the allergen? Although JJ was there, he's at the bottom of my suspect list. Just to cover all bases, I'd let Nowak talk to him, assuming he'd talk to her.

When I pulled in front of Maggie's house at 2222 Harmon Street, the road was empty save for a gas company truck two houses down. The faded blue stucco house had overgrown hedges, and the lawn was nothing more than a patch of weeds littered with trash. Stepping on the porch, I saw a lawn chair and a potted plant. A puddle of water welled under the pot, indicating that someone had recently taken care of it. There was no doorbell, so I knocked. I waited a few minutes and then knocked again. No one answered.

The window blinds were pulled down. I'd been in houses similar to this. A bunch were built in the mid-1950s: small one-story cheap tract homes. Tiny living room in front with two bedrooms and a bath off a hallway. Kitchen in back.

After walking through an opening in the chain-link fence to the rear of the property, I peeked in the back window. The kitchen looked in order; no dishes sat on the counter or table. There was a small dinette with two chairs. A coffeepot, a microwave, and a prescription bottle sat on the countertop. A medium-sized duffel bag was stacked on a cardboard box near the darkened hall entrance. I couldn't see much past that. I'd return here tomorrow unless I heard from her before then.

My cell rang.

"Hi, Sergeant, this is Elias."

"What can I do for you?"

"My sister just got a hold of me, and I told her about our conversation. She said she has nothing to hide and wants you to meet her at her house tomorrow morning at eight. Can you do that?"

"Sure."

Leaving Maggie's house, I headed over to the precinct. On the way there, I called Nowak to update her.

"I agree with you. The dealer seems the most likely suspect. But you're right. There doesn't seem to be any connection between her and my uncle. And JJ seems unlikely as well, but I'll talk to him."

"I'm going to do some more digging around to see if I can uncover a link between them. I'm meeting her at her house tomorrow morning at eight."

"I'll meet you there," Nowak offered.

I gave her the address. "I'm heading back to the station now."

"Sergeant, have you reconsidered the possibility that my uncle's killer is already in custody?"

"Yup." And that thought killed me.

CHAPTER 24

"Why would Norman keep the EpiPen? It doesn't make any sense. If he committed murder, the first thing he would've done was get rid of the evidence." I sat opposite McFalls at his desk.

He pushed his chair back. "Criminals are stupid. That's why."

"What about the pattern of oil on the cards?" I continued. "Ray's cards had the most concentration of it."

"One theory is that after Norman rubbed oil on Ray's glass, Ray then transferred it to his cards." McFalls stretched his arms overhead.

I had to let him know that I'd seen the results without getting Beaker in trouble. "Most of the residue was on the front of three cards. The same three cards Ray had."

"Oh? How do you know this?"

"I took a look at the evidence."

"Did you get assigned to my case without me knowing?"

"No."

"Listen. Norman admitted making all the drinks that night and easily could've messed with Ray's glass." McFalls paused. "José, I've got this. We're covering all the bases here. I get it. Norman is a friend of yours, and you don't believe he did it."

"No, I don't. Do you want to know my theory?"

He massaged the back of his neck. "Sure. I'll hear you out."

"What I think is that the dealer held the deck with oil on her fingers and the oil rubbed off on the sides of the other cards as well." I watched McFalls carefully for any sign that I might be onto something. His facial expression remained in a neutral state, eyes unblinking, forehead relaxed. I could tell he was unmoved by my theory.

"We interviewed everyone who was there that night. The dealer only met Ray that evening. She had no motive, but Norman did." He glanced at his computer screen. "On another note, I'm sure you heard by now we got the ballistics report back from the shooting on River Street. It was from the same gun that killed Officer Cory Palmer fifteen years ago. The gun we weren't able to find at the time."

My stomach dropped and my pulse sped up. "Do you think Ray's death could be connected to that? His work convicted the perp, even though they didn't have the weapon."

"Ray's work on that case led to the killer's lethal injection."

"I know." I rubbed my temples at the start of a tension headache. "Think about it. The same gun that was never found in the old cop killer case was used to shoot at Nowak and me. Doesn't that make you think there has to be a connection to what happened to Ray?"

"No. I don't think so. Because the shooter's mask we found in the trash leads directly to gang activity. Plus, we don't know if they were aiming at you or at someone else." McFalls slid open a drawer, extracted two wrapped yellow candies, and handed one to me. "Bottom line, Ray was killed with peanut oil, not a bullet. Which brings us back to Norman, who had a syringe full of it in his possession. My team is covering all our bases. This case is at the top of my pile; I will make sure it gets all the attention it needs."

I couldn't write the gun off. It had to have something to do with Ray's death. I unwrapped the lemon candy and popped it in my mouth. I remembered Norman telling me he had lost twenty pounds by running. He was about the same height and weight as the shooter. For a split second, I played with the thought the two were the same and then dismissed it. Norman had no reason to kill me. "What I don't get is why, after all these years, the gun shows up, right after Ray's killed. Then it's aimed toward me, who's been asking questions about his death. That's not random."

"Gangs use all types of guns and get them anywhere they can. You know that as well as I do."

"Yeah. But what concerns me is the timing of it all. It's way too coincidental."

"I agree. The chain of events seems like a solid correlation. But right now, the gang unit doesn't think it is. I get that you want to help your buddy. But you're connecting dots that aren't even on the same page." McFalls stood. "Aren't you supposed to be on vacation this week, visiting your family in Miami?"

"Yeah, I'm leaving soon." Or maybe not at all, depending on how long it took me to find answers.

"We've got this covered. Go enjoy your break and leave this case—*my case*—alone."

He was not mincing words. Although he'd heard me out and listened to my theory, he was shutting me down. "Sure. I've just got a few things to clear up on my desk."

"José, for what it's worth, I'm really sorry about your friend Norman. I know it's hard for you to accept that a buddy of yours could be a cop killer."

"No kidding."

After logging into my computer, I pulled up the Tiburon/ARS system. It was my first go-to when trying to find information about someone. It combined dispatch calls, information from police reports, addresses, telephone numbers, birth dates, and more.

When I typed in "Margaret Linzey," assuming Maggie was her nickname, nothing came up. I tried different spellings of her first name. Still nothing.

Typing in just "M. Linzey" also produced nothing. Maybe she

had a license issued in another state. Elias had mentioned that she'd lived in Vegas. I sent an email to the Nevada driver's bureau, inquiring about Margaret "Maggie" Linzey. Hopefully, it wouldn't take too long to get a response.

After a quick check in the reverse directory database, nothing came up on her cell number. A stirring deep in my gut put me on alert. As far as records, it seemed that Maggie didn't exist.

Trying another database, I typed in her address. A few minutes later, I read that the 2222 Harmon Street house had been deeded from Jennie L. Welsh to William Taylor. Searching online for Jennie Welsh, I found her obituary from fourteen years earlier. It wasn't the normal write-up, indicating who had predeceased her, nor did it list any relatives. Instead, it stated only her birth and death date. Another search listed Jennie L. Welsh as a long-term patient in a local psychiatric residential treatment program.

I called the treatment program. After being transferred to three different people, I was finally put in touch with an employee who could help me.

"Jennie L. Welsh died fourteen years ago while she was a patient at your facility. What can you tell me about her?" I asked.

"I'll check my database. Can you hold for a moment?" After a long pause, she came back on the line. "She had been a patient here for a year leading up to her death."

"What led her to be a patient at your facility?"

"She was admitted due to a mental breakdown. Ms. Welsh had acute stress. It manifested itself in depression and dissociation, where she was no longer able to function on a day-to-day basis. There are notes that she also had severe paranoia and schizophrenia."

"What caused the breakdown?"

"Losing her nineteen-year-old son."

"He died?"

"No. Incarcerated." She gave me his name.

I jotted down David James Welsh. His name sounded famil-iar. I would have to confirm, but it sounded like the name of the guy who'd just had lethal injection for killing Officer Cory Palmer. The hair stood up on the back of my neck. The very gun from that shooting had recently resurfaced, and the cop who'd put him away for it was now dead. There had to be a connection. "What crime did David Welsh commit?"

"I can't find it in the notes."

His mother was dead. He was now dead. Maybe it was one of his relatives who'd sought revenge. "Did she have any other children? Family? Spouse?"

"Let me see." She paused. "One other son. Aaron Thomas Welsh. He was seven years younger than David."

Then Aaron had been twelve years old when his brother had been sent to prison and his mother admitted to the psych ward. That would make him twenty-seven years old now. Could it be David Welsh's brother who'd killed Ray? "What happened to Aaron when his mother was admitted?"

"That I'm not sure. There are no other relatives listed on her intake forms. No spouse or other family. Since he was a juvenile at the time, I assume he went into foster care."

I'd look Aaron up. Although finding information on a minor was often challenging, I needed to find out where he was now. "How was Jennie treated for her condition?"

"Therapy and medication."

"How did she die?"

"Inpatient suicide. She hung herself in her room." There was a long silence. "We monitored her closely, did a suicide risk assessment, like we do on all patients. The staff here is highly trained, and we follow all necessary protocol. But sadly, it still occurred." Her voice choked.

"I'm not here to judge you," I assured her.

"After her death, we came under close scrutiny. Every detail was looked over to see what we could've done to prevent it. We've since put many safeguards in place so nothing like that could happen in the future. Sergeant Rodriguez, if there aren't any more questions, I have to get to a meeting."

"I appreciate your taking time to talk with me."

"You can email or call me if you need anything else." She gave me her email address and cell number.

Back on my computer, I typed in "David James Welsh." This brought me to a recent article in the *Savannah Morning News*, which began, "Condemned cop killer David James Welsh, who was convicted in the shooting death of Officer Cory Palmer, was executed by lethal injection…"

A few days after the lethal injection, Ray had been killed. Then a day later, I had been caught in gunfire, shot at by the same weapon that had killed Palmer. Ray was the cop who had put away David Welsh. The hairs on my arms stood on end. This was not happenstance. This was a solid association.

Who could have wanted retaliation? There was only one living relative of David Welsh. His brother. I typed in "Aaron Thomas Welsh." I tried several searches and found nothing on him.

If Maggie had killed Ray, as I suspected, then she must be connected in some way to David. Maybe Maggie was David's girlfriend, or wife? A friend, a neighbor? There had to be a connection. Right now, there were loose ends that needed to be tied up.

And who was William Taylor, the current owner of Jennie Welsh's home? I uncovered that William had been given the deed to her home in probate court because he was her heir.

Her heir?

As far as I knew, her son Aaron was her only living relative. How was William connected to her? Had Aaron changed his name? He'd been twelve years old when his mother had been institutionalized and his brother incarcerated. And his mother had died shortly after she had been committed. Aaron must've gone into foster care, since there were no other family members to take him. Perhaps he'd been adopted and changed his name?

It was the only theory we had that made any sense. A brother killing the cop who'd put away his sibling. And the brother on death row had triggered his mother's enormous trauma, leading to her mental breakdown and taking her away from him.

Aaron had lost everything, which in turn could compel him to seek revenge. Looking into every available database yielded no answers as to what had happened to Aaron Welsh. He had to be out there. Where was he now? And how was he connected to Maggie?

From what I surmised, Maggie was renting the house from William Taylor. I couldn't find a contact number for him.

Searching for Elias Linzey's name resulted in nothing. Not finding either sibling in the database could mean any number of things. First, people who were trying to hide something often gave a false name. Second, it could be that they were from another state or county and thereby wouldn't come up in my database. Third, it could be as simple as that they had never had any sort of contact with the police.

The question burning in my mind was why I couldn't find Maggie or Elias in the system.

For the next hour, I investigated online to find answers. My searches amounted to nothing more than what I already had. I knew that at eight tomorrow morning, I would meet Maggie at her house. Maybe in talking to her, I could determine whether or not she'd had any reason to kill Ray. Or at least I could find out if she knew Jennie, Aaron, or David Welsh. My gut said there was an association, and that relationship was the clue to who'd killed Ray. Meanwhile, I would be cautious in case she was setting me up.

My thoughts on the Welsh link and Ray nagged me to no end. Where was Aaron, and how was Maggie involved in all of it?

A text chimed in from Regina. "You are *my lucky star*. There'll be a cute single guy there tonight I want you to meet. Make sure that you *express yourself*." I cringed, knowing that all her Madonna song references were meant to encourage me to live my life as an openly gay man.

Like Bezu, Annie Mae, and Cat, Regina didn't think my reasons for keeping my sexuality secret were valid. Thankfully, they all respected my decision although they never gave up trying.

The duplicity I led kept surfacing. Such as when I got fixed up on a date when I knew, but could not admit, there was no chance I'd have a romantic relationship with the woman. The guilt and deception were overwhelming.

My secret was hurting others and my career.

More than ever, I was tired of lying to myself, to my family, and to my peers. It was tearing me apart. With the secret, I was only half living. But when should I come out? And more importantly, was I ready for the repercussions of that decision?

CHAPTER 25

"*I*'m glad it wasn't too much effort for you to find something to wear." The sarcasm in Regina's greeting was not lost on me as I entered the party.

She wore a white lingerie wedding dress, fingerless lace gloves, several necklaces, and white pumps. Her hair was puffed in a big eighties hairstyle, her lipstick red, and her eye makeup dark and heavy. I recognized the iconic Madonna look from the 1984 MTV awards.

"Hey, I'm here, and I'm wearing a costume." I made a check-mark motion with my finger in the air. "One favor checked off the IOU list."

She grabbed my forearm and tugged me through the throng gathered in the back courtyard as Michael Jackson's "Billie Jean" blasted from the speakers. The smell of charcoal-grilled hamburgers wafted in the air. Lights strung through the trees canopied the crowd in a soft white light.

I bumped into someone dressed as Prince who was followed by a guy dressed in a ripped tank and blond mullet wig like an eighties version of wrestler Hulk Hogan.

Out of the corner of my eye, I spotted a guy around my age standing by the bar. He was wearing a letterman jacket, T-shirt, faded jeans, and running shoes. He had shoulder-length layered brown hair, although I wasn't sure if it was real or a wig. He looked like Mel Gibson's character, Riggs, from *Lethal Weapon*. His high cheekbones looked familiar.

Our eyes locked for a moment before I turned away. I felt a stirring of attraction but quickly submerged it as Regina began to introduce me to her friends.

"Glad you made it, José. Nice to see you, Regina." Beaker, my buddy from forensics, handed us each a beer. "I've made myself the unofficial greeter and drink-getter here."

Beaker wore a dark brown fabric-brimmed hat, and a whip hung from a belt loop on his khaki cargo pants, which were tucked into dark boots. He wore a button-down shirt under a tattered leather jacket. His face was sponged with dark brown makeup to simulate stubble.

"You look exactly like Harrison Ford," I claimed.

Beaker beamed. "I wonder if it'll help me get Cyndi Lauper over there to notice me."

"I happen to know her; I'd be glad to make an introduction for you," Regina offered.

"Um, why I, um…" Beaker's face flushed.

"I'm taking that as a yes." Regina took hold of Beaker's leather jacket and pulled him with her as she walked away.

"Ponch, huh?" I heard from behind me.

I turned and saw the guy I had locked eyes with earlier. "Yup. And you're Riggs?"

He stuck out his hand. "Earl Chu."

I recognized his name. But with the costume, he looked nothing like the straight-laced attorney I'd seen in court or helping Norman during his recent murder interrogation. "José Rodriguez. Nice hair."

"I have to say, I rocked the same style back in high school. Not sure the look would work in my day job."

"You're an attorney. I've seen you around. You're defending Norman Sanders?"

"Yup. That's me."

"I hope you can prove his innocence."

"I'm doing my best. I saw you the other day outside the courthouse talking to Patrice DeLeon. I assume you're friends?"

I shrugged, giving a noncommittal answer. It was a loaded question with too much bad history.

"Anyway, you might have already heard, since rumors fly around Savannah quicker than gnats show up on a summer day —she resigned," he told me.

"Yeah, I heard that."

He leaned in toward me. "Between you and me, the council has appointed me to fill the casual vacancy. It hasn't been announced yet, so if you can keep it our secret, that would be great."

His sharing a confidence with me felt intimate, and I liked the feeling. "Congratulations."

"Thank you." Earl smiled. "By the way, that same day I saw you with DeLeon, there was also a pretty blond lady you were with. Wife? Girlfriend? Significant other? Or just one of your many admirers?"

"Why does it feel like you're stalking me?"

"Guilty as charged." He laughed. "So, you don't want to answer my question? That's fine."

My throat constricted. Was he fishing around in order to find out if I was straight? Single? "She's a friend. I'm single." Why in the hell did I just say the "I'm single" part? Why hadn't I stopped at "friend"? The information had seemed to roll off my tongue without passing through my brain. I cringed inwardly.

"Oh, good." He grinned and nodded. "I've been wanting to talk to you for a while, but there never seemed to be a good opportunity until now. It's nice we finally got to meet, even as Riggs and Ponch. Maybe we could grab a bite to eat sometime as our real selves?"

Had he just asked me out? I was taken aback by his boldness yet felt flattered at the same time. Was that last line, "our real selves," a reference to my hiding my sexuality? Before I could give him some lame answer, like "No, that wouldn't work."

Regina approached us.

"I'm glad you found each other. I've been wanting you two to meet," she declared.

I felt hugely uncomfortable, as though all eyes were on me. Changing the subject, I asked her, "How did Indiana Jones and Cyndi Lauper do?"

She pointed to a table, where Beaker sat talking to a young lady in an orange-red wig. "They seem to be hitting it off just fine."

"If you two would excuse me, there's someone I need to talk to. José, you can let me know your answer later. I'll be here all night." With that, Earl left.

"What was that about? What answer?" Regina tapped my arm.

"Nothing." I felt the heat of embarrassment rise in my neck.

"I can tell you're hiding something. He asked you out, didn't he? José and Earl sitting in a tree," she whispered in a singsong voice. "He's been asking me about you. You know he's openly gay, right?"

I felt cornered and pissed off. When I decided to, I'd come out. It would be in my time, on my terms. Not because I'd been forced. And dating out in the open was way, way out of the question. "I'm getting another drink. I don't think you need one, as you're drunk with meddling in people's lives."

"José, I'm really sorry I pushed. You know I only want the best for you, that's all." Her smile faded.

"Apology accepted." For the remainder of the night, I avoided Earl, and later that evening, I snuck out without anyone noticing.

Tomorrow morning, I would get some answers from Maggie. Answers I hoped would lead me to Ray's killer.

I knew I had a sleepless night ahead of me, but I'd rather face that than give Earl an answer to his proposition.

CHAPTER 26

*A*fter parking my SUV in front of Maggie's house, I took
in the area. Three cars were parked across the street.
None were in front of her house. It was five minutes to eight.
Nowak confirmed that she was on her way to meet me here. I
poked my head around the corner of the house. No cars were
parked around the other side. And her moped wasn't there,
either.

Maybe I had arrived too early.

As I walked up the steps, I saw the front door was cracked
open. I knocked and announced through the small opening,
"Sergeant Rodriguez from the Savannah Police Department,
here to interview Maggie Linzey."

I waited a couple of minutes. No answer.

Proceeding with caution, I slowly opened the door a few
inches wider and announced myself again. I stepped one foot on
the doormat. Immediately, the door caught on something. Stop-
ping, I craned my head to see that the door leaned on a trip wire
and there were also wires coming out from under the doormat.
The same wires led to a gallon of gas and a battery.

Shit. A bomb. *I was set up. Damn it. I wasn't careful enough.*

Which meant that Maggie knew I was onto her. And she

wanted me dead before I could catch her. I'd been right. Maggie had killed Ray. Where was she now?

I assessed my current situation.

There had to be a pressure-sensitive trigger under the door-mat, as well as a trigger that ignited as the door pushed open and tightened the wire. There were several wires, but my eyes followed a white one that I believed, if cut, might disarm the IED.

My chest constricted and my heart rate increased. I stayed exactly where I was and took in some long, calming breaths. I knew that moving the door either forward or backward could cause the trigger to activate. I was stuck. Even reaching into my jacket to grab my cell phone could set off the bomb sequence.

"Good morning, Sergeant," Nowak said.

"Not so good of a morning here. There's an IED, and if I move an inch, I could trip it." I kept my voice steady and calm, although my heart pounded in my ears.

"Are you kidding me?" Nowak came up behind me, enough for me to see her face as I looked out of the corner of my eye. Her face looked pale, and her eyes were wide.

"Let me walk you through this. Just like we've practiced countless times, okay?"

"Fine. Yes. Okay." Her voice was shaky. "What the heck? I mean, this means that Maggie is—"

"First, call for backup. Second, secure the area. Make sure no one is around. Then, go way across the street out of harm's way until backup arrives."

She made the call, and then I heard footsteps leaving the porch. Good. For once, she was listening to me. If this went sideways, I wanted to be the only casualty. No innocent bystanders. Especially not Nowak.

Thinking that my life could end right here, right now, made me terribly sad. I hadn't lived my life in truth as I should have. I didn't care anymore if everyone knew I was gay. If I got out of this alive, I would be real and let the chips fall where they would. In this moment of crisis, the thought of continuing to live a lie was worse than the thought of any repercussions my truth might cause.

Shoving those thoughts from my mind, I refocused on the task at hand.

I kept my foot on the mat and the door exactly where it was. If I could get to the detonator and cut the wire, I thought it would disarm. Once the bomb squad got here, they would be able to take care of this in no time.

My arm began to tingle with the loss of feeling as I held the door exactly where it was. I didn't even want a breeze to push it open because that could set off the bomb. I felt a bead of sweat drip into my eye, but I couldn't wipe it away. A car door slammed behind me. As much as I wanted to look, I didn't dare. Remaining perfectly still was the only way to keep the pressure exactly the same and the bomb intact.

I heard Nowak's voice coming from *inside* the house.

"I've got this. I'm going to take care of this." Nowak reached the living room, adjacent to where I was stuck at the door with one foot on the doormat. She must have entered through the back door.

"No. Damn it! I said wait for backup, and that's an order." She was just as stubborn and bull-headed as Juanita.

She knelt next to the IED and opened her toolkit. "If you go, I go. We're in this together. There's no changing my mind."

Anger seared through me. "You directly disobeyed an order. I'm going to write you up. Kick you off the squad. Unless you leave *now*," I threatened.

"Go ahead. I don't care." She flashed a light at the wires. Her forehead creased in concentration.

"Well, I do." Rage and fear roared through me. The last thing I wanted was for anything to happen to her. I heard car doors slamming and voices behind me. The bomb squad had arrived. "You're insubordinate."

"There's a timer. We don't have a second to lose. If you're done scolding me, I'd like to tell you my strategy. Right now, this"—she pointed to a cluster of wires, the white one in particular—"is the wire that needs to be cut to disarm the bomb. I'm sure of it. I need to prove to you that I know what I'm doing. Now is as good a time as any."

Footsteps on the wooden porch sounded behind me. "Stop. Backup is here."

She pulled out clippers and snapped the wire. "Too late."

Her impatience was her downfall. Thankfully, her bomb disarmament skill was her salvation.

Our salvation.

CHAPTER 27

"*I* heard your rookie Nowak did a great job disarming the bomb; she must have had a great teacher," McFalls said as we stood in Maggie's house.

"Thanks. She's still a little rough around the edges, but in time that will smooth out, too." I smiled. I was proud of her, although I was aggravated she hadn't followed my direct order. She'd have to work on that. I'd told her as much before she'd left to go back to the precinct and research Elias and Maggie. "Have you found Maggie Linzey yet?"

"No. She seems to have disappeared into thin air," McFalls observed.

"Did you call her brother, Elias?"

"Yes. And we couldn't reach him, either. I have an officer at the Magnolia Club now, hoping Elias shows up to work."

"I doubt he's going into work. There has to be another way to find him. He and his sister must have planned all this." I scanned Maggie's living room again, trying to see if we'd missed anything. There had to be something here that could lead us to them. I had already checked out all the evidence that had been bagged, but couldn't find from it any indication of where they might be now.

"Getting them in custody is our number one job," McFalls

agreed. "I hate that any jackass can find out how to build a simple bomb using household items and a few things from the local hardware store. These things are all over the Internet." McFalls rubbed his forehead. "I hate the Internet."

"I hear you. We have to deal with homemade IEDs all the time."

"I'm glad this worked out okay. I hate that this whole thing could have turned out way differently."

"That's why we're here. To protect people from things like this."

He exhaled. "We'll find Maggie and Elias, trust me on this. I've got a whole team after them."

"Good. In the meantime, I'm going to look around the house one more time. See if we missed anything."

"Suit yourself. I'm heading out." He began to walk away but then stopped. "You know, this whole time you've been trying to tell me there was more to the case. Although you pissed me off with your interfering, I think I owe you an apology."

"No need. We're good." I grabbed plastic gloves and evidence bags. I entered the bedroom and searched the dresser, nightstand, and closet but found them empty. I checked under the bed, dresser, and rug. Lifting the mattress, I didn't find anything stashed under it.

In the bathroom, I looked behind and inside the toilet tank as well as the medicine cabinet.

Afterwards, I made my way into the kitchen. I rummaged through the refrigerator and then through the kitchen drawers. Under the kitchen sink, I pulled out a trash can that had already been emptied by McFalls' crew.

Sticking my head under the sink, I pushed aside an assortment of cleaning supplies and saw a small *empty* prescription bottle tucked way in the back corner behind a bottle of Comet. I grabbed it.

It was from the local pharmacy and had been prescribed to William Taylor. The medicine was Sumatriptan, which I recognized as migraine medication. It had been filled one month ago —thirty tablets, with one refill left. The bottle being empty meant that William needed a refill soon. Or that he might have already gotten one. I snapped a picture of the label and then bagged the bottle.

My first thought was that Elias and William Taylor were the same person. They had to be. There was a strong chance not only that Elias was really William but also that William had once been named Aaron Welsh. After his mother had been admitted to the psychiatric hospital, he'd been put in foster care. Sometime after that, he could have been adopted and changed his name. Or he could have changed it when he'd come of legal age and left the foster care system.

Either way, my hunch was that Elias and William were the same person. I texted Nowak about my theory and asked her to do research on it.

The house had been deeded from Jennie Welsh to her heir, and Aaron was her only heir, as her other son had been on death row when she'd died.

Following this line of thought, if Elias was Aaron, he had every motive to kill Ray.

But how was Maggie involved in all of this? That was the missing piece. Had Elias set Maggie up to work at the poker tournament in order to kill Ray? How had Elias known Ray was allergic?

Looking back, I remembered seeing Ray at the Magnolia Club when I'd been there for Sweetie Pie's performance. Elias had placed a bowl of snacks in front of Ray, which had ended up spilling on him. Ray had pulled out his EpiPen and made a scene about being allergic. Elias had witnessed all of it. He could easily have told Maggie this. Somewhere along the line, he found out Norman needed a dealer and he'd volunteered his sister.

However, Aaron/Elias didn't have a sister. He had a brother, David. Or maybe he had someone he considered a sister from foster care or an adoptive family?

Another possibility was that Elias *was* Maggie. Norman transformed himself into Sweetie Pie, a pretty believable drag queen. Elias could've easily done the same transformation with makeup and clothing. Maggie and Elias had a similar build, tall and slender.

I'd seen Maggie wince a few times during the night of the tournament and put her fingertips to her temples. It could've been that her head was hurting. Elias suffered from migraines, as well, which made my theory even more plausible.

Elias, as an employee of the Magnolia Club, had access to the dressing room. He could've entered Norman's dressing room without anyone taking too much notice. He could have put the EpiPen filled with peanut oil into Norman's makeup bag. As Maggie the dealer, it would have been easy for him to replace Ray's real shot with the tampered shot during the poker tournament. And in turn, he could have made sure the cards dealt to Ray received the most oil in order to cause an allergic reaction.

The gun. Elias might very well have known where his brother had stashed the gun used to shoot Officer Palmer. It was all lining up.

He killed my coworker, framed my friend for murder, shot at Nowak and me on River Street, and had tried to blow me up today.

I needed to find Elias, or whoever he really was, *myself*.

It was personal.

CHAPTER 28

*a*s I left Maggie's house, I made a call to McFalls with an update on my train of thought regarding Elias and his connection to Ray.

"Vengeance is a powerful motivator, no doubt. I agree with you: Elias lost his brother and mother, and he must've blamed it all on Ray," McFalls concurred.

"Which is twisted thinking, because his brother committed murder, and Ray was just doing his job," I added.

"I know. But no matter how Elias tries to hide, I've got officers all over town looking for him. We'll find him," McFalls claimed. "I issued a BOLO. He might have skipped town."

A 'be on the lookout,' also known as an all-points bulletin, would be sent through dispatchers to police officers across our jurisdiction, neighboring jurisdictions and even across country. In it would be details about Elias, his aliases, age, height, and weight. However, I felt that he was still in Savannah.

I knew that Elias would not show up at the Magnolia Club. He would know that was the first place the police would look for him. And he would not dare go back to 2222 Harmon Street. He had already cleared it of his personal belongings, expecting it to be destroyed.

The only place that seemed reasonable for him to make an

appearance was the pharmacy where he could get his meds. Unless he had a way to get them elsewhere, or would do without.

On the other hand, he could have taken off right after he'd set the bomb and be long gone by now.

"If you don't mind, I'm going to the pharmacy to see if Elias picked up his prescription," I said to McFalls.

"No need. I'm sending an officer over there," he assured me.

"Why don't you let me go?"

"José, I would. You know that I appreciate your help on the case, but—"

"Let me do this," I persisted.

"Something tells me that you're planning to do it anyway, with or without my approval."

∽

"I WONDER IF YOU COULD HELP ME OUT." I SHOWED THE pharmacist my badge. "Has William Taylor refilled this prescription yet?" I showed him a picture of the label.

"Let me see." The pharmacist searched his computer. "No. He hasn't. But it's filled and ready for him to pick up."

"How late are you open today?"

"We close at five."

"Thanks." It looked like I was in for a two-and-a-half-hour observation.

There were two employees at the front of the store, working the registers, and one pharmacist with two assistants in the back. Five workers. A college-aged kid with a candy bar and chips was getting rung up at the register. An elderly couple was in the back near the pharmacy, occupying two of the six chairs in the waiting area. They sat next to a table stacked with magazines.

A mother, holding a toddler on her hip and carrying a shopping basket with diapers, walked past me. I hoped they would all be leaving soon. It would be better not to have any civilians around when Elias showed up. But there was no way I could control who went in without drawing attention to myself and potentially scaring away Elias.

As I left the pharmacy to do a perimeter check, I called Nowak to get her up to speed on everything.

"Not that it matters now, but I did as you had asked and talked to JJ. He had no motive." She paused. "I want to do the stakeout with you," she announced.

"No. I'm doing it solo." The back door of the building was locked, with a key access code needed to enter. An area with a wooden fence housed a small dumpster. Four employees' cars were parked in the back. A gas station was on the left, a bed and breakfast to the right. Behind the pharmacy was an alley, and beyond that a row of townhouses.

"If you don't mind me saying, you're stubborn, Sergeant, sir," Nowak told me.

"I do mind." I hung up and jogged to my vehicle. I'd parked it in a lot across the street from the pharmacy with a clear view of the front door. I got in my car and pulled out binoculars from my glove box to do a spot check. Two cars were parked next to the automatic door of the building, one in the handicapped spot. A lime-green bicycle was chained to the bike rack on the left side of the building near three empty shopping carts.

A few minutes later, the college-aged kid unlocked his bike and rode away. The elderly couple got in their Buick, which was parked in the handicapped spot, and also drove away.

A half hour after that, a car pulled up next to me. Nowak got out and knocked on my window. I shot her the evil eye as I lowered the glass. "What part of *solo* didn't you understand?"

"Are you going to let me in?"

"No." My neck tensed. She had a knack for pushing my buttons. "Leave now. That's a direct order."

"I'll just sit here in my car next to your car."

"You'll do no such thing. *Go*."

"I want to get my uncle's killer. I *need* to be here." Her eyes pleaded. "C'mon, Sergeant."

I understood why she wanted to be here. It was personal to

me, too. But I couldn't put her in danger again, as had happened at Maggie's house. "No. Final answer."

"Then I'll just go in the pharmacy and wait." She crossed her arms over her chest.

She was impossible. I pushed the unlock button. "Get in and keep quiet."

"But I have to talk so I can tell you what I found on the research you wanted me to do."

"Fine."

"So, I called in a few favors at the courthouse to get some quick answers. Bottom line, your theory was correct." She paused. "When Aaron Welsh turned eighteen, he legally changed his name to William Taylor. So that means that the cop killer my uncle put on death row was his brother, David Welsh. It all adds up now. Elias must be William's alias."

I then explained why I thought Elias was Maggie.

"Yes, that makes sense, too." She slumped in the seat. A tear streaked down her cheek. "Knowing this doesn't bring back my uncle."

"No. I'm sorry."

She sniffed. "But at least we can put away his killer."

"That's all we can do." Going back to my line of sight on the business, I noticed Annie Mae's car pulling into the pharmacy parking lot. I called her cell phone. "What are you doing?"

"I'm running errands," Annie Mae answered. "Want to grab dinner later?"

"I can't. I'm working."

"I thought you were on vacation."

"I am."

"I don't know if anyone ever told you, but working and vacation don't go together."

I let out a forced breath.

When Elias showed up and things went sideways, I didn't want Annie Mae anywhere around. "Listen, can you get in and out of the pharmacy quickly?"

"How did you know I was here?" Annie Mae asked.

I grumbled.

"Are you doing surveillance on this store?" She whispered, "Is it a drug ring with prescription meds or something? Ooooooh, can I help? Please, pretty please?"

"Yes, you can."

"Yeah?" Her voice rose. "What can I do?"

"Leave the building."

"No, I mean really help. Who you looking for?" Her voice was low and quiet. "No one can hear me. I'm being very stealthy by the snack aisle. I'm not going anywhere. I'll be your eyes inside here."

Now I was dealing with two obstinate women. It was best to get her off the phone. Hopefully, she'd get bored and leave before Elias showed up. If he showed up. "Do you remember the bartender at the Magnolia Club?"

"Yeah. He made me a great margarita."

"If you see him inside the pharmacy, text me. But I still strongly suggest you get what you need and leave. *Quickly*." With that, I hung up.

"I overheard. You've got someone on the inside now?" Nowak asked.

I groaned as I looked through the binoculars. The mother with the toddler got into her minivan. Good. All that remained inside, for now, was five employees and Annie Mae.

Nowak continued, "I've never had migraines, but I hear they're horrible. If I had that kind of intense pain and medicine helped, I guess I wouldn't want to be without it. But why didn't he pick up his medicine before he tried to blow you up? I have some thoughts on that."

I looked away from her, hoping that got across I didn't want to hear her suppositions.

"I bet when he knew you were onto him, he had to act quickly, making the bomb and all. He didn't have time to think about his meds. Or maybe he couldn't refill it early. I know insurance is really strict on that." Nowak sank into the seat.

My neck tightened in irritation. But part of me also filled with pride. She was making valid, logical deductions.

I continued to observe the building, taking note of vehicles as well as pedestrians and cyclists passing by. Thankfully, no one else had entered the business.

"Another possibility. I bet he wanted to get out of town right after the explosion, but he couldn't because he needed to pick up his pills. Bet he plans to leave town right after he gets them."

Nowak was asking and answering her own questions, having an entire conversation with herself. Just like my sisters, who could talk to a wall.

Despite my amusement, it concerned me to no end that both Nowak and Annie Mae were here. I couldn't live with myself if anything happened to either one of them. To anyone. I needed to make one hundred percent certain that everyone was safe and protected.

I continued surveying the area.

I hated doing nothing. I wanted Elias caught. Put behind bars. Norman released. Justice served. This all wrapped up. Maybe, just maybe, still have a few days to spend in Miami with my family.

An hour later, a moped pulled in front of the pharmacy. A person wearing a hoodie and who had the same shape and build as Elias got off the vehicle.

The back of my shoulders tensed as my heart race increased.

It was showtime.

CHAPTER 29

"*T*arget walked in," I texted Annie Mae as I got out of my vehicle. "Get out."

She texted. "No, bossy. I'm staying. Got him in my sights. Definitely the same guy who served me the drink at the club. He's heading back to the pharmacy."

I texted Annie Mae, "Leave now and don't make a scene."

Annie Mae texted back, "I'm being casual by the nail polish rack. Do you think blue sparkly color is in? Or is that too trendy?"

"EXIT NOW. GO." I hoped that all caps emphasized how serious I was.

"Stay put," I said to Nowak as she opened the car door.

"Are you sure?" Her legs swung out of the car, but she kept one hand on the door.

My body stiffened. "Call backup."

"Okay." Nowak slid back into the car but kept her hand on the handle.

"I mean it."

She released the handle. "Fine. I'll stay out here and make sure that if anything goes down the area is secure."

I ran across the street. The humidity and heat left the air with a smell of thick, murky marsh water. Thankfully, traffic was light, and the only pedestrians were down the block. If Elias was armed, which I suspected he was, I wanted to know who and what was in the area in case of gunfire.

Annie Mae texted, "I'm a big girl, in more ways than one. You don't have to baby me. I'll be fine. I'll text you when he leaves."

It was no use trying to get Annie Mae to go away.

I put my cell on vibrate and tucked it into my pocket while keeping my focus on the pharmacy's front door. I made my way toward the front of the building. As I passed the moped, I regretted that I didn't have time to disable it. Besides, he might notice me then. Meanwhile, I decided to wait outside the front door for him, so that no one inside would be trapped.

I leaned against the outside wall and waited for him to exit. I knew that approaching him outside left it easier for him to get away. It also increased the possibility that innocent bystanders might get caught up in any altercation, or worse, fall into the crosshairs of bullets. I didn't want to take that chance, either. My gun was in my waistband holster over my right hip. My hand hovered over it.

I stepped back a few feet, out of the direct view of the automatic sliding glass doors but still able to keep my eye on the surrounding area.

Taking in a long breath, I settled into a focused alert state, calming my mind. Training and experience had prepared me for all kinds of scenarios, but in reality, there were no absolutes. Anything could happen.

Clearing my head was critical. Not losing concentration was essential. Every time a bird chirped, a vehicle drove past, a breeze brushed branches overhead, I took it all in while maintaining my focus on the door. I knew that Elias could exit at any time.

I felt as tense as a spring pulled taut. Every cell in my body stood at attention.

My phone vibrated. Not wanting to look away from the door for even a second, I didn't pick it up, instead assuming it was a text from Annie Mae telling me our target was on the move.

I clenched and unclenched my hands.

Seconds later, the door whooshed open.

I pressed my back against the side of the building, feeling my spine against the jagged bricks as my eyes remained locked on the walkway in front of the door. I needed to make sure it was Elias before I reacted.

He came into my line of sight wearing a dark hoodie pulled over his head. He held a bag in one hand and keys in the other as he walked briskly to his scooter and slung a leg over the seat. As he did, I noticed a telltale bulge in his pant leg. He had a gun. Thankfully, the area was clear of civilians.

Like a panther waiting on its prey, I sprang in front of him with my gun drawn, "Get on the ground. Show me your hands."

His eyes went wide as he fumbled to turn the key in the ignition.

Fury raged in me. He was not getting away. Not on my watch.

I jumped on him, knocking the moped on its side. A searing pain raced down my arm from the impact of my shoulder hitting the metal frame. Elias let out a grunt as he crashed to the ground with the moped on top of him. Wriggling out from under it, he cussed.

He reached in his pant leg and yanked out a Glock 19. When I kicked at his arm with all my force, Elias fell backward and the gun dislodged from his hand, skidding with the rattle of metal on cement across the pavement toward the bike rack.

Annie Mae emerged from the building. She picked up the gun and aimed it at Elias. "This is why you don't carry a weapon. It can be taken and used against you."

I lunged at Elias and yanked his arm as he attempted to scramble to his feet. Using my bulk, I body-slammed him to the ground. With a thud, he was down. I wedged his belly to the pavement and jerked his arms behind him while reading him his Miranda rights.

Elias was all muscle and rather strong for being half my weight on a slight physique. He put up a fight, wrestling and twisting under me like an alligator trying to get loose.

I struggled to hold him down.

There was no way I would ever let him get free.

Two unmarked cars sped to a stop and parked in front. Backup had arrived.

"Aaron, it's over," I said.

"Why didn't you just blow up like you were supposed to?" he yelled.

"I guess that wasn't in the cards for me, *Maggie*."

Elias spat.

"And another thing—you owe my buddy Norman an apology," I grunted.

He let out a muffled remark.

"To show you what a nice guy I am, I'll make sure you have your migraine medicine with you in prison," I claimed.

Tension drained from me as officers surrounded us. Nowak stood among them. When she caught my gaze, she gave a thumbs-up.

We got him. He wasn't going anywhere but to the penitentiary. The man with four names, Aaron, William, Elias, and Maggie, would now be known by a number.

"To think you told me and the girls to stay out of police business." Annie Mae approached. "I guess this means that we shouldn't listen to what you say."

CHAPTER 30

Six Months Later
Miami, Florida

"This is my mom and dad," I said to Earl. "And, Mom and Dad, this is my partner, Earl."

My father, back stiff, lips tight, stuck out his hand and shook Earl's outstretched one. I wondered if it felt as awkward as it looked.

"You are such a handsome man." My mother wrapped Earl in a bear hug. "Do you like arroz con pollo?"

Earl's eyebrows rose questioningly.

"It's chicken and rice," I laughed.

"Then, in that case, yes, I do," Earl chuckled.

"Come with me; I made some today. You sit down and have a bowl. It's not too spicy. Cuban food is good. You'll like it." My mother guided him toward the back of the house. "José's sisters and their families will be over later," she continued as they disappeared into the kitchen.

"So, Dad, are you sure you're okay with this?" I sat down on the overstuffed sofa that creaked under my weight. "I mean, you've only had a few months to get used to the idea."

My father took the seat next to me. "Son, you know me. I'm what they call old-style."

"Fashioned." I grinned.

"Yes." He folded his hands on his lap. "You know, it is going to take time for me to get used to all of it."

"I get it. I do." I leaned forward and put my elbows on my knees. "But I couldn't continue living a lie. Mostly to myself. It wasn't working for me anymore to pretend to be someone I wasn't."

My dad looked straight ahead as he gave a slight nod.

"All this time, I convinced myself that I would be ostracized at work. That everyone was homophobic, and it would negatively impact me. You know what?"

My dad shook his head.

"In the end, it didn't matter. It turned out I was the one judging them, not the other way around." I paused as I thought about Ray's volatile relationship with his father, and how his father hadn't attended Ray's memorial. "A bigger dread than telling my coworkers was telling you. I thought for sure you'd disown me. And worse, that you wouldn't be proud of me anymore. Give up on me."

"*No te salva ni el médico chino.*" He flipped his hand open.

"Yes, I thought there was no hope for me."

My dad looked at me. "Son, I could never throw away you or any of my children. But this secret you told us? It's all new to me. I don't know what to do with it. But you are still my son." His voice shook. "And I am outnumbered by women telling me what to do."

"Yeah, Mom and my sisters are a persuasive bunch, huh?"

He nodded. "Four against one. I didn't have good odds. But they insisted I open my mind to your—what do you call it? —*lifestyle.*"

"I could barely accept it myself, let alone expect you to." I looked around the living room. The same family pictures hung on the wall. The furniture was unchanged and still arranged as it had been since my childhood. When I took in a deep breath, the house had the same familiar aroma of garlic, onions, and spices. "Thank you and Mom for inviting Earl to join me here."

"Juanita's idea."

"Go figure." I smiled.

"We missed you. It's good to have you home." He cleared his throat. "You never made it here last time like you were supposed to."

"I'm sorry. Like I told you, I had a lot going on."

He waved a hand as though wiping a spot in the air. "I know. I know. You arrested a bad guy, got promoted to lieutenant, busy busy. Too busy for family."

"Dad, I'll always make time for family. You have my word on that."

He reached out and set a hand on my knee. "Son. I might not understand boy-and-boy dating. But what I do know for sure is that I am proud of you. That I am *certain* of."

And I was positive that was all I needed to hear.

BOOK 5: *PUZZLED BY PURPLE* COMES OUT IN 2019! TO RECEIVE an email when it's available—along with updates on the book's progress and other news about my novels—be sure to sign up for my free author newsletter at **loislavrisa.com/newsletter**.

ACKNOWLEDGMENTS

Any story starts with an idea and then grows from there. Along the way, many people helped and supported me as I turned my idea into a finished book. First and foremost, thanks go out to my husband, Tom, and our four incredible children: Sean, Melanie, Tiffany and Ryan.

To my many writer friends for the great ideas, encouragement, critique, review and counsel. In addition, to all of my friends who listened to me while I plotted out my stories and talked about characters (as though they were real), thank you for letting me bend your ear. Your input has been extremely valuable in making this book better.

ALSO BY LOIS LAVRISA

Liquid Lies

GEORGIA COAST COZY MYSTERIES

Dying for Dinner Rolls

Murderous Muffins

Homicide by Hamlet

Killing with Kings

Puzzled by Purple

To purchase, please visit loislavrisa.com/books, or head to your favorite online bookseller.

ABOUT THE AUTHOR

Lois Lavrisa grew up on the rough and tumble South Side of Chicago. She earned a Master's and Bachelor of Science in Journalism and Communication with a minor in Public Relations. After college, she wrote training programs for a Fortune 500 company, taught many years as an adjunct professor, and was also a professional cheerleader for the Chicago Bulls. She's been married to her aerospace husband Tom since 1991 and they have four (nearly grown-up) children—two sons and two daughters.

Lois's first novel, *Liquid Lies*, was a finalist for the 2013 Eric Hoffer Award. For her Georgia Coast Cozy Mystery series, set in beautiful historic Savannah, Lois was nominated for Georgia Author of the Year.

To get the latest news on Lois's books, be sure to sign up for her free author newsletter:

www.loislavrisa.com/newsletter

facebook.com/authorloislavrisa

twitter.com/loislavrisa

instagram.com/loislavrisa

CPSIA information can be obtained
at www.ICGtesting.com
Printed in the USA
FSHW021952120819
60991FS